CW01560556

ACKNOWLEDGMENTS

Thank you as always to my rock, Jean, I'd be lost without
you in my life.

Special thanks as always go to @studioenp for their superb cover
design expertise.

My heartfelt thanks go to my wonderful editor Abby, my proofreaders
Joseph, Barbara and Jacqueline for spotting all the lingering nits.

Thank you also to my amazing ARC group who help to keep me sane
during this process.

To Mary, gone, but never forgotten. I hope you found the peace you
were searching for my dear friend.

ALSO BY M A COMLEY

Blind Justice (Novella)

Cruel Justice (Book #1)

Mortal Justice (Novella)

Impeding Justice (Book #2)

Final Justice (Book #3)

Foul Justice (Book #4)

Guaranteed Justice (Book #5)

Ultimate Justice (Book #6)

Virtual Justice (Book #7)

Hostile Justice (Book #8)

Tortured Justice (Book #9)

Rough Justice (Book #10)

Dubious Justice (Book #11)

Calculated Justice (Book #12)

Twisted Justice (Book #13)

Justice at Christmas (Short Story)

Justice at Christmas 2 (novella)

Justice at Christmas 3 (novella)

Prime Justice (Book #14)

Heroic Justice (Book #15)

Shameful Justice (Book #16)

Immoral Justice (Book #17)

Toxic Justice (Book #18)

Overdue Justice (Book #19)

Killer Blow (DI Sara Ramsey #2)

The Dead Can't Speak (DI Sara Ramsey #3)

Deluded (DI Sara Ramsey #4)

The Murder Pact (DI Sara Ramsey #5)

Twisted Revenge (DI Sara Ramsey #6)

The Lies She Told (DI Sara Ramsey #7)

For The Love Of... (DI Sara Ramsey #8)

Run For Your Life (DI Sara Ramsey #9)

Cold Mercy (DI Sara Ramsey #10)

Sign of Evil (DI Sara Ramsey #11)

Indefensible (DI Sara Ramsey #12)

I Know The Truth (A psychological thriller)

The Caller (co-written with Tara Lyons)

Evil In Disguise – a novel based on True events

Deadly Act (Hero series novella)

Torn Apart (Hero series #1)

End Result (Hero series #2)

In Plain Sight (Hero Series #3)

Double Jeopardy (Hero Series #4)

Criminal Actions (Hero Series #5)

Regrets Mean Nothing (Hero #6)

Sole Intention (Intention series #1)

Grave Intention (Intention series #2)

Devious Intention (Intention #3)

Merry Widow (A Lorne Simpkins short story)

It's A Dog's Life (A Lorne Simpkins short story)

Cozy Mystery Series

Murder at the Wedding

Murder at the Hotel

Murder by the Sea

Death on the Coast (April 2021)

A Time To Heal (A Sweet Romance)

A Time For Change (A Sweet Romance)

High Spirits

The Temptation series (Romantic Suspense/New Adult Novellas)

Past Temptation

Lost Temptation

Tempting Christa (A billionaire romantic suspense co-authored by Tracie Delaney #1)

Avenging Christa (A billionaire romantic suspense co-authored by Tracie Delaney #2)

PROLOGUE

*S*he thrashed around in her bed, aware that she wouldn't be able to change things, not now, not ever.

She'd had the same recurring nightmare over and over for years.

Megan wiped the sweat from her brow and began fanning herself with her quilt. She leapt out of bed and carried out her daily stretches, easing the tension and the kinks out of her weary body. *Yet another mostly sleepless night which invariably ended with the same nightmare. When will they end?*

It was the same question she'd asked herself hundreds of times over the years, since that tragic night had devastated her life. Sleep had become progressively hard to come by lately. She was shattered most days and had resorted to catnapping when at all possible, like today. The time was four-thirty, and she was on course for what lay ahead of her. Her great loss never far from her mind. The life she'd once had shattered with a click of the fingers. She felt so alone now, so distraught most days when the memories surfaced.

Lifting the medium-weight dumbbells, she carried out several reps, working her upper arms until the muscles complained. Then she jumped in the shower.

Mild exercise helped clear the sadness from her mind and replaced it with fortitude. She blow-dried her blonde locks and tied them back. After selecting the appropriate coloured wig, she fixed it in place and admired her image. She'd made the right choice this time, brunette with subtle red tones suited her down to the ground.

The next dilemma she had to deal with was to choose a suitable outfit to wear. She slid the wardrobe door open and studied the array of clothing up to the task. Primark had recently had a sale on that had proven to be too good an opportunity to miss out on. A thought struck her. She sidestepped to the chest of drawers and opened the second one down, flipping aside countless garments until she found the particular one she had in mind. A sexy lacy black bodice. She grinned and held it up against her slim frame. A wicked smile replaced the grin as yet another thought emerged.

She riffled around in another drawer and located something she thought would work a treat for what she was proposing. She fastened the extra padded domes into the bodice and slipped into it. Laughing, she turned sideways to check out the transformation. Within seconds she'd gone from a thirty-two A to a thirty-six double DD. "I could get used to this," she muttered. "Some women pay extortionate fees to a plastic surgeon to achieve this look. Why bother going under the knife in the first place?"

After selecting a low-cut blouse from her wardrobe and a black above the knee skirt, her ensemble was complete, almost. She dug around in the bottom of the wardrobe for the strappy sandals she'd bought as a mistake, hoping they would come in handy in the future. Well, that time had now arrived. She slipped them on and once again admired her image from every angle.

"Sexy bitch! You'll do, for what I have in mind." Megan spent the next five minutes practising her sensual walk in front of the mirror. Slow and steady, that's the key. Not long after, she gathered her sequinned evening bag, filled it with her purse, phone and keys then left the flat. Her movements now driven by the revenge pulsating through her veins.

She jumped in her car, aware of what she must do to prevent anyone tracing her movements later, once the deed was done. Megan drove to the location, ensuring she parked a few streets away from where she was about to meet her… date.

The preparation she'd carried out ensured she walked steadily in her heels. She entered the pub under the watchful gaze of the customers already there—two men at the bar, a group of men at a table in the corner and another group of more mature women on the bench seats in front of the bay window. The barmaid appeared from the back room and smiled at her as she approached the bar.

"Evening, what can I get you?"

"Hi, any chance of a cocktail?" she asked tentatively.

The barmaid frowned. "I can get you anything you like, I might have to ask Google how to concoct something I've never heard of, but I'm up for the challenge. What's your poison?"

"A Mojito or a Margarita perhaps?"

"I can make both of those, which do you prefer?"

"Let's stick with the Mojito."

The barmaid hunted around under the counter for a few minutes, cussing now and again. Eventually, she resurfaced, looking pleased with her achievements as she held up the metal cocktail shaker. She got to work creating the drink. Megan hopped up onto the stool and removed her coat.

The rest of the punters got back to their conversations. Megan could see out of her peripheral vision that one of the men standing at the bar kept glancing her way in between taking large gulps of his pint.

Brimming with satisfaction, the barmaid poured the Mojito into a cocktail glass she'd sourced from the bottom shelf which she rinsed and dried first. She presented the drink and added a straw for that special touch. "How's that?" She smiled, appreciative of her own achievement.

"Looks fine to me, it's all in the taste though. How much do I owe you?"

"I'll get that," shouted the man who'd been scrutinising her since she'd arrived.

She fluttered her false eyelashes at him. "Oh no, I couldn't possibly allow that, but thank you all the same."

"Nonsense. I said I'll get it. Put your money away. Tracey, come here."

The barmaid raised her hands. "Hey, I'm keeping out of it. It's up to you, sweetheart. What do you want to do?"

Megan sighed and offered the man a broad smile. "If you're sure? I'm quite willing and able to pay my own way."

The man left his seat and picked up his pint, he took five paces and joined her. "I'm certain. Can't have a beautiful young lady like you drinking on her own now, can we?"

"Who says I'm alone? Maybe I'm waiting for my husband or boyfriend to arrive. Perhaps they're late."

He took a step back. "Sorry, have I got the wrong end of the stick?"

Megan frowned. "It depends on what you mean."

"I thought you were alone, out on the town... umm, looking for some company."

She sniggered. "In that case, you're a very astute young man. I was only winding you up." She patted the stool beside her. "Here, take a seat. Tell me all about yourself."

His serious expression gave way to one of relief. A dimple appeared in his right cheek as he smiled. He slipped onto the stool next to hers and slid a ten-pound note across the bar to the barmaid. "I'll have another pint while you're at it, Tracey."

The barmaid cocked an eyebrow, crossed her arms and stared at the tenner. "Umm... not until you give me more money, the cocktail was eight quid, Jason."

He jutted his head forward. "What? Bloody hell, I hope it's worth it," he mumbled.

Don't you worry about that, Jason Davis, mark my words, it'll be totally worth it!

"Don't feel obliged to pay for my drink, I told you, I'm not averse to paying for my own drinks."

But he insisted, "No, I never go back on a promise. You can get the next round, how about that?"

She shrugged. "Suits me."

Tracey supplied him with another pint of beer and left them to get acquainted. The conversation flowed easily enough. At one point, Megan almost had regrets about fooling the man sitting beside her. He seemed a decent chap, compared to the other men who had taken an interest in her over the years.

"So, Melinda," he said, using the false name she'd supplied him, "what do you do for a living? Wait, don't tell me, let me guess." He placed a finger against his cheek and tapped it. "How about a model?"

"Wow, you've hit the nail on the head at the first attempt. How did you manage that?" She glanced down at her cleavage and chuckled. "Oops, never mind, I think I can guess. And yes, I'm a certain type of model."

He raised a finger. "No, don't tell me. I'll take a punt and say you model wellies and rainwear. How did I do?"

Megan laughed. "Appallingly, I model underwear, but you figured that out all by yourself, you were just pulling my... leg, weren't you?"

He leaned in and pecked her on the cheek. "I was. Hey, we're getting on like a house on fire, aren't we?"

"Why do you sound surprised when you say that?"

He shrugged. "To look at you, I'd say you were out of my class, just goes to show, doesn't it?"

"Perceptions can be deceiving, as I know to my cost."

He inclined his head. "What do you mean? Not trying to pry or anything."

She waved away the suggestion. "It's fine. Ignore me. The last thing I want to do is go all maudlin. I'm having a whale of a time, it would be a pity to spoil things now."

"If you're sure. Do you live around here?"

"Yes, not too far," she replied, intentionally omitting the area she lived in just in case the barmaid was earwigging their conversation.

"This is my local. I've been coming here for years."

"And your wife puts up with you spending a lot of time here?"

"Oh, I'm not married. Far from it, I love my freedom too much."

Liar!

She glanced down at his hands to see his wedding ring slip off his finger and heard it clatter onto the bar under his palm. "Oh, my mistake. You," she hitched up a shoulder, "seem the married type."

"Nah, not me. What about you?"

She waved her ringless hand around. "Young, free and extremely single. Still waiting for my Prince Charming to arrive. They appear to be few and far between these days."

"That's a shame, I would've thought a pretty girl like you would have been snapped up long ago."

"Flatterer. I had a ring on my finger once, when I was engaged to Tim…" her voice trailed off and her head dipped on purpose.

He covered her hand with his. "What happened? Go on, we're friends, you can tell me."

"He was killed in a crash. Joy riders with nothing better to do with their time."

His hand slipped from hers and she distinctly heard him gulp. "That's terrible. I'm so sorry to hear that."

His words sounded genuine enough, but she was aware they were just that, words. Her story might have been made up, but there was a snippet of truth involved. Her mood had turned sour. She needed to cast the past aside and concentrate on the present.

Revenge! It was enticingly within her grasp now.

"See, I told you I didn't want to get maudlin, ignore me. It happened years ago, I'm over it now."

"You don't seem over it. Mind you, how do you get over something as dreadful as that?" He twisted his glass on the bar.

"You have to. Life goes on. Anyway, tell me more about you. What do you like to do in your spare time when you're not working as a painter and decorator?"

His head shot around to face her. "How do you know what I do?"

Shit! She was forced to think fast on her feet and ran a finger down the paint ingrained in his knuckles. "Umm… call it a lucky guess."

He laughed. "Bloody gloss paint, it's a devil to get out of the crevices sometimes."

"I'm sure. Do you enjoy your work?" she asked, relief flooding through her.

"Mostly, it can get a little mundane; I suppose that's true of any job, right?"

"Of course. I get bored with taking my clothes off and jutting my breasts out at the camera twelve hours a day most of the time."

"Wow, I thought you'd love it. Don't most models revel in all that attention from the camera?"

"It's not as glamorous as most people think. I spend the majority of the day undressed, which is fine when we're in the midst of a heat-wave, not so good in the middle of December, I can tell you."

"I never really thought about it. Poor you."

"Never mind, at least the money is good. Want another?"

He downed his drink and rattled his glass on the bar to gain Tracey's attention. "You've twisted my arm."

They spent the next hour or so chatting. It was a comfortable encounter and one that made her hesitate for the slightest moment when it was time for her to leave.

"I have to go now. It was lovely meeting you. I'm afraid I have an early shoot in the morning."

"That's a shame. Maybe I can drop you home?"

"That would be wonderful. Hang on, how many have you had?"

"Three, maybe four. It's fine. If you live locally, it shouldn't take me long to drop you off."

"Go on then. I'd like to spend more time with you. I've had a fun evening."

He hopped off his stool and helped her off hers. "It's been a fabu-lous evening." He tucked her arm through his, waved at Tracey and they left the bar. He stopped at a Nissan Pathfinder and opened the passenger door.

"Why, thank you, kind sir. What a big… car you've got."

He chuckled and ran around the front to jump in the driver's side. "Where to, m'lady?"

"I'll tell you the way."

He drove out of the car park and followed her instructions. She led him to a bit of wasteland she knew down by the River Thames. He cut the engine and rubbed his hands together then turned in his seat to face her. His grin of expectation rankled her. She stabbed the needle into his leg and released the clear liquid before he had a chance to react. The serum rendered him incapable of either moving or saying anything.

Megan went to work. She tied his hands and his ankles, well-practiced in what knots to use for effectiveness. His eyes, wide with fear, followed her movements.

"You're an evil bastard who deserves what's coming to him. As if I could ever be interested in you after the way you destroyed my family. You make me sick. You and the others will be punished, all of you will perish before the week is out. You can all join up in hell and joyride to your hearts' content with no fear of ruining others' lives the way you've wrecked mine."

His eyes widened and followed her out of the car. She opened the driver's door and pushed a button. Then she rushed to the back of the car and removed the fuel cap. She withdrew a ten-inch piece of material she had in her pocket, lit a match, and placed the material into the tank and stood back. Then she ran to the front of the vehicle and watched the terror in his eyes until finally his body was engulfed in flames as the car exploded.

Removing her shoes, she ran towards the alley off to the left and slowly made her way back to her vehicle which was parked a few streets away.

One down, three more to meet their fate!

*K*aty woke with a start, tore out of the bed and raced along the hallway to her daughter's bedroom. Georgie was sound asleep. She inched closer to listen to her breathing; it was steady, nothing to worry about, this time. This had been her routine several times a week since Georgie had been rushed into hospital almost three months earlier. Even though the doctors had assured her Georgie was now out of immediate danger, she could do little to push down the rising panic that emerged every so often to taunt her. The doctor had been certain that Georgie's immediate future would be secure and said that they intended to monitor her closely in case things go awry. He'd told them that most kids with a heart defect were resilient. The odd exception to the rule would need surgery to correct the faults which showed up. Although, his final words had chilled her to the bone. There was no telling what kind of damage the meningitis had done to her heart, if any, and it might take months for them to find out.

She knelt beside her daughter and swept the fringe out of Georgie's eyes. AJ appeared in the doorway and asked in a panicked voice, "Is she okay?"

Katy glanced his way and nodded. "I think so. It was just my vivid imagination working overtime."

"Thank God. Come back to bed, let's enjoy the peace and quiet while we can."

Katy kissed Georgie's temple and walked out of the bedroom. "I'll go make us a coffee. I should be getting a move on soon anyway."

AJ went back to bed. She rejoined him with toast and coffee ten minutes or so later. She'd just settled back into bed when her mobile juddered across the bedside table. She picked it up and through a mouthful of toast said, "DI Katy Foster."

"Sorry to disturb you, ma'am. It's Mick."

Katy rolled her eyes at AJ and mouthed an apology. "I know it has to be important for you to be calling me directly, Mick. What's up?"

"We've been dealing with a nasty one since first light that has your name written all over it."

"My personal name? Or is that your way of saying this case is right up my street?"

"Sorry, yes, the latter."

"Okay. You're telling me I need to get my arse into gear and get to the scene, aren't you?"

"Yes, actually, the pathologist just called in, wondering where you were."

"Patti? Okay, if she's chasing my tail, it must be a bad one."

"It is. Shall I call her back to tell her you'll be with her soon?"

"Hang on a sec, you haven't told me what the location is yet."

He sighed, and she heard him flick through a couple of pages before he gave her the address.

She quickly assessed how long it would likely take her to get dressed and drive the short distance to the scene. "Okay, tell Patti to expect me in around thirty minutes. Tell her to bear with me because I'm actually not even dressed as yet."

"Oops, again, I apologise for disturbing you so early."

"There's no need. See you later." She ended the call and ripped into her piece of toast.

"Why you? Can't someone else attend and you pick up the slack later?"

She cocked an eyebrow at her husband and took a sip of coffee. "If only it worked like that."

"I know, wishful thinking on my part. Anything I can do to help?"

"Nope. I'll shove this down my neck, have a quick shower and make a dash for it. What have you got on today?"

"Several contacts I need to chase up. One party to start organising, and the rest of the day will be spent scouring the area for extra bookings. I'm not stressed about it, word of mouth is getting around and the phone never stops ringing with enquiries. I'm lucky in that respect."

She leaned over and kissed him. "Have I told you lately how proud I am of you?"

He glanced at the clock. "Ooo… it's been at least ten hours, but yes, carry on piling on the praise."

"You're amazing. To have stumbled across something that could make us a lot of money in the future."

"Hold your horses. The business is still relatively new; saying that, I'm delighted by the amount of success we've had so far."

"*You've* had. All your success is down to your sole input. Who knew kids' parties could be so lucrative?"

"I had an inkling, otherwise I wouldn't have *entertained* the business." He chuckled. "See what I did there?"

Katy groaned. "It hadn't gone unnoticed. I'd better get my arse into gear."

"What you need to do is finish your breakfast first."

She gulped down the rest of her toast and coffee while she sorted through her wardrobe. The navy trouser suit caught her eye. She teamed it up with a white blouse and then raced into the bathroom and jumped in the shower.

Twenty minutes later, she'd kissed AJ goodbye and was on the road. She rang her partner en route. "Hi, Charlie, did you get the call?"

"Morning, boss. Yes, I'm almost there. How about you?"

"Another ten minutes, depending on traffic, it's not been too bad so far."

"It was all right at my end, it's too early for normal folks to be on the road."

"Okay. I'll see you shortly."

Katy ended the call and put the radio on to ease her through the rest of the journey.

*P*atti was retrieving some equipment from her van when she pulled up beside her vehicle. Charlie joined her. "Morning, ladies. Sorry for ringing you so early. Thought you'd want to get cracking on this one right away."

"No need to apologise, I'm used to you disturbing my sleep." Katy grinned.

"As long as that's all I was disturbing."

Katy sighed. "Yep, old married couple now. Early morning hanky-panky went out of the window years ago."

"Shame on you, Katy Foster... it is still Foster, isn't it?"

"Yes, at work. We thought it best to keep things as they were. Enough about me. Should we suit up?"

"Always wise. I hope you've got a strong stomach this morning, it ain't pretty."

"Are any of them?" Katy moved to the boot of her car and dug around for a couple of suits. "Umm... supplies are getting low back here, just saying."

Patti took the hint and returned to her vehicle. She collected a couple of paper suits and handed them to Charlie. "These might be of some use to the pair of you."

"Gee, thanks, Patti. What would we do without you?" Katy called over. "It's okay, I have an abundance of shoe coverings."

"So glad to hear it. Come on, get a wriggle on, ladies. I haven't got all day."

Once they had slipped on their protective suits, gloves and shoe coverings, Katy and Charlie followed Patti to the scene. The technical team were hard at work, collecting evidence from the burnt-out vehicle.

"I'm taking it this was intentional, bearing in mind the location being off the beaten track?" Katy surmised.

"Yep. I had my doubts for the tiniest moment, but now I'm pretty sure this was down to someone with a seriously cruel agenda."

Katy tilted her head and moved closer to the car. "Single occupant. Any wounds that you can tell?"

"Not as such, apart from the man roasting in the car," the pathologist replied sarcastically.

"Okay, so someone torched the car and killed him, I agree, that's pretty cruel."

Patti shook her head and walked over to hold up an evidence bag. "We found traces of rope inside."

"Rope? As in he was bound?"

"Yep. Someone tied him up and then torched the vehicle."

"Ouch! Not good news. Have we got an ID on the victim?"

"Nothing that I can give you for definite, always difficult when there's fire involved as you can imagine. The plate is intact, so that's a bonus."

"Charlie, can you do the honours for me?" Katy asked.

Charlie fished out her mobile and placed the call. She waited for someone back at the station to feed her the information and then hung up. "Jason Davis. I've got his address for when we need it."

"Does he live far?" Katy asked, surveying the rest of the scene before moving on to the surrounding area.

"Not too far. About five minutes by car, that's an estimate on my part, of course."

"Okay. What else have you got for us, Patti?"

Patti folded her arms, her paper suit rustling as she tapped her foot. "Not a lot at present. I'll know more once we get him back to the lab and opened up."

"In the meantime, I suppose we'd better go and see if there's a next of kin at his address. Wait, who called it in?"

"A postie stumbled across the car at around five this morning."

"Must've been a shock for them. Keep in touch, Patti, the sooner we get on with the onerous task of informing the relatives, the better."

"Good luck. I don't envy you in the slightest. I'll be in touch soon, although it might take me a little longer than normal to file the report."

"I know you'll do your best. TTFN."

Katy and Charlie walked back to their respective cars. Katy tapped the postcode into the satnav and told Charlie to follow her to the location.

a woman in her early forties opened the door to them. "Oh God, he's not... dead, is he?"

"Mrs Davis? I'm DI Katy Foster and this is my partner, DS Charlie Simpkins, would it be okay if we came in to speak to you?"

She inched the door closed a little. "I'm not sure. Answer my question first."

Katy inhaled a large breath. "If you're talking about Jason Davis, then yes, I'm sorry, we believe he's dead, although his true identity has yet to be confirmed."

Mrs Davis staggered backwards and slumped against the wall in the hallway. Katy ran to assist her. "No... no, this can't be true. It can't be. Sammy... Sammy, come down here."

A younger woman with long blonde hair appeared at the top of the stairs. "Get away from her. Who are you? What are you doing to my mother?"

Katy and Charlie produced their IDs, and the girl ran down the stairs to inspect them. "Oh shit! I'm sorry. I didn't mean to mouth off like that." She turned to face her mother and reached out to her. "Mum, what's going on?"

"It's your father. They're saying... he's dead." Jane Davis sobbed.

Her daughter pushed Katy aside. "If you don't mind, I'd like to comfort my mother. Is he? Dead, I mean?"

Katy took a further step to the left. "Why don't we go into the lounge or somewhere more comfortable to discuss this?"

Charlie closed the front door. Sammy indicated which room to enter and they all headed that way. Sammy supported her mother whose body was limp with grief.

After the four of them were seated, Katy relayed what they knew regarding the incident.

"What if it's not my father? Do you really think you should come here telling us that he's dead if you haven't identified him yet?"

"We have no reason to think it's not him. He was found in his vehicle which is registered to this address," Katy replied, wondering how the young woman would know such a thing.

"I'm studying criminology at university. I'm home for a break at the moment."

That explains it! "Ah, I see. I'm sorry to add to your grief, but I need to ask a few questions about your father's whereabouts the last few days. If that's okay?"

Mrs Davis nodded at her daughter. "They have to do their job, love, let them get on with it, all right?"

Sammy closed her eyes and let out a large sigh. She opened them again and said, "Dad was a frequent visitor at the local. Mum and Dad had a row last night, he stormed off to the pub and never came home."

"Was it a regular occurrence? Him staying out all night?"

"Yes, he's been known to sleep in either his car or his van on occasions. That's why neither of us reported him missing."

Katy nodded. "Ah, I did wonder. Can you tell us which pub he usually used?"

"The Fallow Deer Inn, a few streets away," Sammy told them.

"Why did he take the car and not walk, if it's that close?" Katy enquired.

"You'd have to ask him that, oh wait, you can't, because he's bloody dead!" Sammy sneered. "What type of question is that?"

"I'm sorry. I just need to get more background into your father's actions, et cetera. Some of the questions I'll be asking might seem a little idiotic, but please bear with me."

"If we must," Sammy grumbled.

"He always took his car. The number of times I've tried to dissuade him, is nobody's business," Mrs Davis added. "He was a law unto himself most of the time. Nothing I said could sway his decision making, so I gave up years ago."

"Has he been under any kind of stress lately?" Katy pressed on.

"No more than usual. Work is hit and miss at present, hasn't got back to where it was before that damned virus struck."

"What line of business was he in?"

"He was a painter and decorator. Don't look around, I know you can't tell."

"Don't worry, we're not here to judge. And he used the same pub all the time? It was his regular, was it?"

"Yes. He trundled down there at least four nights a week. I've pleaded with him to knock it on the head as money is tight, but me opening my mouth only appeared to make him more obstinate. No man likes to be told what he can and can't do, do they?"

Katy smiled. "I suppose. To your knowledge, has he fallen out with anyone recently?"

Sammy squeezed her mother's hand and asked, "Why? Are you saying he died in suspicious circumstances?"

"Unfortunately, yes."

Both women gasped and tears slipped down Jane's cheeks. Sammy flung an arm around her mother's shoulders. "Stay strong, Mum. Don't crumble now."

"I can't deal with this. I know I didn't always show it, but I loved the bugger. I can't bear the thought of him being killed. Why? Why would someone want to kill Jason? He's never knowingly done anyone any harm, not that I'm aware of. Oh, God, what the hell is going on, Sammy? Why us? Why now?"

"You heard her, why us? Why Dad?" Sammy was quick to fire at Katy.

"It's very early into our investigation, far too soon for us to figure out the whys and wherefores, I'm sorry. Hence my need to come here today and question you. I know the timing could be better, but the more you can tell us about Jason's character and what he got up to, the more likely we are to find the person responsible."

"My dad always had a secret side to him."

"Sammy! You can't say that. What on earth will the officers think?"

"It's okay, Mrs Davis, we need to hear the facts. Secretive? In what way? By that I mean regarding a specific topic or just all round secretive?"

Sammy lowered her head a little and sighed. "You might as well know the truth. Mum and Dad didn't get along."

"Sammy! We did so... occasionally. Although I must admit... recently, his foul moods have made all our lives intolerable. I still loved him, no matter what anger he showed within these walls."

Katy tilted her head. "Are you telling us that his moods developed into something more? Did he abuse you?"

Sammy's head lowered a farther few inches and her mother turned to her and patted her on the hand. "I think we should tell them the truth, sweetie, don't you?"

Katy sensed the women were about to share some interesting news. "Anything you can tell us at this point could prove crucial in our investigation."

"I can't, Mum. Not yet. I need to know how he died first."

Katy nodded. "If you feel you're strong enough to take it. Your father was tied up in his vehicle and someone set fire to the car."

"Oh shit! Was he... burnt alive?" Sammy demanded, her eyes blazing with fear.

"We won't know the true extent of what really happened until the pathologist has completed the post-mortem."

"Why did you have to ask that, Sammy?" her mother asked, horrified.

"It's my warped mind, Mum, I need to know the ins and outs."

"What good will it do to know how he died?" Jane held up a hand when Sammy went to answer. "No, I don't want to hear what goes on in that head of yours. It's full of secrets just like your father's, I'm sure of that."

"That's a bit harsh, Mum, and totally unfounded. Jesus, I'll go and leave you to deal with the police then, I know when I'm not wanted."

Jane clenched her daughter's hand with both of hers. "No, I didn't mean anything by that, I promise. Stay here, I need you to be with me, not upstairs by yourself."

"Okay, it doesn't alter the fact you've lashed out and hurt me though."

"I'm sorry, that wasn't my intention, Sammy. Please forgive me, I'm not thinking straight, not with your father's death."

"All right, but stop having a go at me because of his failings, you've been guilty of doing that a lot lately and I hate it. I'm not him. He was a one-off."

Her mother touched her daughter's cheek. "Again, I apologise if I've said anything harsh lately. We've all been under a huge amount of stress, 2020 was a devastating year for everyone, especially those who are self-employed."

Katy watched the interaction between mother and daughter with interest.

Sammy gave a short, abrupt laugh. "Ha, right, it didn't stop him going out four or five nights a week to piss it up the wall though, as soon as the pubs were open again, did it?"

"Sammy, don't speak like that about your father. Go, leave us alone, don't you think I'm going through enough stress as it is right now without you being intent on slagging your father off?"

"Sorry, it's the truth, whether you want to admit it or not, Mum."

Jane jumped to her feet and pointed at the door. "Get out. Now!" she shouted, shocking everyone in the room, especially her daughter.

Sammy's tough exterior crumbled in front of their eyes. She burst into tears and dashed out of the room, slamming the door behind her.

Jane buried her head in her hands and sobbed. "Jesus, why does she always have to test the boundaries? Now look what she's done. She's forced a wedge between us, just when I need her support."

"Would you like me to have a word with her before we leave?" Katy asked tentatively.

"Would you? No, you have enough on your plate without being a mediator as well."

"It's hardly that. Once we're done here, I'll go up and see her. We'll get you two talking again, I promise."

"I hope so. I'm going to be relying on her for support... once I begin making the funeral arrangements."

"You will. It's never an easy task to handle."

Jane fell quiet for a moment or two. "I didn't have the courage to ask him for a divorce. We should have parted years ago. Yes, I loved him, but I hated him at the same time. Does that sound contradictory?"

"Not in the slightest. The experts will tell you there's a fine line between love and hate. Can you cast your mind back over the last few months, maybe Jason confided in you about feeling fearful of something?"

She shook her head. "No, not that I can recollect. But that doesn't mean to say there wasn't something going on that he felt he needed to keep secret."

"What about his friends? Are they likely to know him any better? Sorry, I didn't mean it to come out that way. Maybe his friends were more aware of what was going on in his life than his family."

"Possibly. He only had one good friend, Nigel Granger. I can get his phone number for you, if you like?"

"That would be extremely helpful. Did your husband go to the pub with Nigel?"

"Now and again. Nigel was more of a homebird, unlike Jason. My husband used to get irate with Nigel at times. Taunted him for being under the thumb, bloody idiot. Just because a man prefers his wife's company to that of his best friend, it doesn't mean he's under the thumb. We had more arguments about that than anything." She left her seat and went in search of her address book. She reeled off the number and Charlie jotted it down.

"So true. Can you think of anyone else who might have likely fallen out with your husband lately? A customer perhaps?"

"No, nothing along those lines. All his customers relied on him to do a good job, he never let them down either. I can't think of anything. I swear, I would tell you if I could. I want this person caught. Wait, what if they come after me or my daughter?"

"Maybe you can both stay with relatives for a few days, just in case. Although I have to say that's probably unlikely to happen."

"But can you guarantee it?"

"No, which is why I made the suggestion to stay elsewhere."

"I'll see if we can arrange that today. I bet that's going to cause another rift between my daughter and myself. She loves the comfort of her home as much as I do, rarely steps foot out of the house except to go to university or to pop round and see her grandparents."

"Maybe you can both stay there, if you're close to them."

"Possibly, can I give them a call, you know, while you're here?"

"Go for it. Why don't I go upstairs and have a chat with Sammy while you make the call?"

"Sounds good to me. Tell her I'm sorry, will you?"

Katy smiled. "Leave it to me."

She left the room and walked up the stairs. At the top, she surveyed the landing and then moved towards the door at the end of the hall when she heard the faint sound of music coming from the room. She knocked on the door and eased it open.

Sammy was sitting on her bed, her legs crossed, listening to her iPod. Katy entered the room and sat on the end of the bed. Sammy's eyes shot open and her hand covered her heart. "Damn, you scared the shit out of me."

Katy smiled. "I'm sorry, I didn't mean to. I knocked, but you couldn't hear me. I hope I'm not intruding, Sammy."

"You are. I don't want to speak to you, or to Mum. I just want today to be over."

"I can understand that. Please, don't shut your Mum out, she's going to be counting on you for support now that your father is no longer with us."

"You reckon? She's always been a hard cow."

Katy tilted her head. "Really? She doesn't come across as uncaring to me."

"I didn't say she didn't care, I said she was hard, emotionally lacking at times. Fails to react like other mothers do when the chips are down."

Katy didn't have a clue what Sammy was going on about. From what she could tell, Jane had reacted normally, if there was such a thing when a family member hears of a loved one's death. "Do you fall out a lot?"

"As she's always reminding me, I'm my father's daughter. We were close, as most fathers and daughters are."

Katy nodded her agreement. The truth was that she and her father had been ultra-close over the years. "I get that. My dad is pretty special to me as well."

"Now he's gone. Our family dynamics are going to alter significantly. I'm not sure I'm going to be able to cope with Mum on my own."

Katy frowned. "Care to tell me more?"

"She's under the doctor for mental illness. Dad abused me when I was ten and she hasn't forgiven herself for letting me down, for not being able to protect me."

"I see. I'm sorry to hear that and yet, you're telling me you were really close to your father."

Sammy shrugged. "Don't ask. It was just the once. He swore he wouldn't do it again. Told me it was a one-off, and I believed him. It was."

"Did your father say why he abused you?"

Her chin hit her chest, and she mumbled, "Because he loved me. I know, I've tried to tell myself that he was wrong, but he was my father, someone I looked up to. I idolised him. Whether he abused me or not, I had his genes running through me. I couldn't cut him out of my life. Mum refused to leave him because of finances, so we had to settle on making the best of a bad job. That's why Dad used to go to the pub all the time."

"That's heartbreaking. How do you think you would have reacted towards your father if your mother had walked out on him?"

"I don't know. I don't suppose I'll ever know, now he's no longer with us."

"Your mother is going to need you now, more than ever."

"I know. I'm too angry right now to be with her. It's not because of what she said, it's in here." She clutched a clenched hand to her breast. "I need to spend the day working through my feelings. I'm struggling to make sense of his death. Strange things keep circulating my mind."

"Such as?"

"What if he was one of those sex pests? What then? What if he touched other little girls up and one of their fathers finally took revenge?"

"It's something that we're going to need to delve into. Did your father ever hint that he may have assaulted another child?" Katy asked compassionately, trying to put herself in Sammy's position, to understand how confused she must be right now.

"No, never. But it's the only thing I can think of as to why someone would want to hurt him... to kill him. He wasn't a saint by any means, is any man? But he didn't deserve to die at the hands of a stranger."

"A stranger or someone he knew, we've yet to figure that out. I promise you I'll get to the bottom of who it was and why they chose to kill your father. Until then, I need you to take care of your mother for me, will you do that?"

"Of course. She knows I'll calm down after a while and forgive everything that was said downstairs. It's what families do, isn't it?"

"Usually, yes. You might want to start packing an overnight bag. Your mother is in the process of ringing your grandparents to ask them if you can stay there for a few days."

"She is? Why?"

"Your mum's worried that whoever killed your father might have plans to stop by and hurt both of you."

Sammy's eyes widened in shock. "No! That can't be right, surely?"

Katy smiled. "Why don't we err on the side of caution and get you shipped out to your grandparents, just in case?"

Sammy shot out of the bed and ran to her wardrobe. She dragged a large holdall off the high shelf and started throwing in some underwear, jumpers and jeans. Her packing was complete within less than five minutes. "Should I pack for Mum as well?"

"Why not? I'll go back downstairs and let her know."

"Thank you for the chat."

"You're welcome." Katy patted her on the forearm and left the room.

Charlie and Jane were chatting quietly in the lounge, and Katy stopped for a brief moment to listen to what was being said. Charlie was consoling Jane and doing a good job of it too. Katy entered the room. Charlie looked up and smiled.

"Everything okay?" Katy asked, her gaze shifting between the two women.

"Yes, I think so. You're going to be fine now, aren't you, Jane?" her partner said.

Jane sniffled and wiped her eyes with a tissue. "I think so. We have to accept he's no longer with us and get on with our lives."

"That's a start. Sammy should be down in a moment."

"Is she all right?"

"I would say she's probably confused about her emotions right now, so give her time to adapt."

"I will. As long as we have each other, I think we'll survive and thrive, now he's no longer around. Over the years I've felt stifled in my own home, does that make sense?"

"You're not the first abused woman to have said that, and I doubt you'll be the last either. My advice would be not to dwell on the past too much, but to look forward. You have a close relationship with your daughter, I can tell that, even though it might seem a little strained at the moment. Give her time to adjust to what's happened. You'll both come through this trauma in the end, I have every confidence in you."

Jane nodded and sniffled again. "Thank you. I believe we're both strong and yes, we will survive. What happens now?"

"The pathologist will be in touch with you soon. Whether she'll give you the go-ahead to view your husband or not is another matter. If she believes his body isn't in a fit state for you to see, then you'll have to accept that's the case, okay?"

"I'm not sure I'd want to see him to be honest, not if he lost his life in a fire."

"When Patti calls you, tell her how you feel. No one is going to force you to do something you don't want to do. There are other ways we can identify him, if necessary."

Jane ran a shaking hand over her face. "Is he really that bad?"

Katy nodded. "Maybe it's for the best if you and Sammy remembered him as he was."

Sammy entered the room behind her and ran into her mother's outstretched arms and hugged her. The two women sobbed and kept apologising to each other. *Time to go, there's nothing left for me to say.* Katy gestured to Charlie that it was time for them to leave.

Jane glanced up and nodded.

Katy waved and placed a card on the nearby table. "Ring me if you need anything."

"We will and thank you," Jane replied.

Katy and Charlie left the house. On the way back to the car, Katy blew out a breath. "God, that was a chore and a half. Mixed emotions flying around. I wouldn't want to be in their shoes over the next few weeks, coming to terms with their wayward thoughts and feelings."

"I'm with you there. It begs the question about what we're up against though, doesn't it?"

"Yep, several possibilities are coming to mind, there's no doubt about that, Charlie. Let's see what the pub's landlord has to say."

2

The Fallow Deer Inn was a newish pub in the middle of a recently erected housing estate. It had an outdoor seating area to the right, and Katy could imagine whiling away a pleasant evening here in the summer with AJ and Georgie. Back to the grim task in hand, she and Charlie entered the public bar to find a man in his fifties with a bit of a paunch on him, standing behind the bar in a conversation with another man of a similar age who was on the other side, drinking a pint of lager.

"Hello, there. What can I get you?" he asked jovially as he walked the length of the bar towards them.

Katy produced her warrant card. "DI Katy Foster and DS Charlie Simpkins, are you the owner or manager?"

"I own this place. What's up? We haven't broken any rules, not that I'm aware of."

"No, it's nothing like that, sir. We're investigating an incident that happened not far from here."

He frowned and scratched his temple. "You'll need to give me more than that. What type of incident?"

"We believe it involves one of your customers," Katy said, evasively.

"Who?"

"Jason Davis, do you know him?"

"Of course I bloody know him, he's more than a regular, he's a close friend of mine."

"Ah, okay. Perhaps you can tell us if he came in here last night?"

"He did. Left pretty early from what I can gather too."

Katy inclined her head. "Sorry?"

"I was off duty, but Tracey said he had his eye on a woman in here last night."

"Is Tracey around?"

"She should be reporting for duty soon. Why? What's Jason been up to now? Apart from the obvious. Always had an eye for the ladies, that one."

Katy sighed. "Sorry to have to share this news with you, but last night, Jason died in an incident."

His head craned forward and his eyes bulged. "What? No way." He gripped the bar with both hands as if to steady himself. "No bloody way. I can't believe I'm hearing this. An incident or an accident, did you say?"

"An incident. We can't really say more at present."

"Why's that?"

"We need to keep the facts about the inquiry confidential in case the press get their hands on anything and scupper our investigation."

His frown deepened. "I'm not with you. Wait a minute! You're not telling me there was foul play to this incident, was there?"

Katy issued a tight smile. "I can't give you more than that, not yet, sir."

"Bloody hell. I know what you're getting at. You're telling me he's been murdered, aren't you?"

Katy shrugged. "I need to ask if you have any cameras in the bar."

He pointed at a few spots in the immediate area. "Take your pick, the place is riddled with them. Want me to search for something for you?"

"If you wouldn't mind?"

"Again, I can't really leave the bar until Tracey shows up." At that moment, a young woman wearing ripped jeans and a tight T-shirt stretched across her ample breasts entered the bar. "Ah, here's my right-hand woman now."

"I wondered why my ears were burning. Talking about me as usual, are you, Stuart?"

"Not in the way you think, love. I've had some devastating news about Jason. These ladies are coppers, they'd like to have a word with you."

Tracey walked behind the bar, placed her handbag under the counter and stood alongside Stuart. "What are you going on about? What news?"

Katy cleared her throat. "Was Jason here last night?"

Tracey shrugged. "He's always here. Why? What's happened to him? Come on, Stuart, I'm getting worried now."

Katy pushed ahead, not giving Stuart the chance to respond. "How long was Jason here?"

"Let me think. Ah, yes, he left earlier than normal with a young lady."

"Do you know the lady in question?"

"Nope, she was a first-timer, not seen her in here before, at all. What did she do? Cut his dick off?" Tracey laughed, her gaze shot between Katy and Charlie, and her laughter died as quickly as it had emerged. "Oh, God, don't tell me I'm right?"

"I can neither confirm nor deny your statement."

"What?" Stuart asked. "Why the secrecy about this? You've told us bugger all and yet you expect us to tell you everything, it works both ways."

Katy gave a taut smile. "I'm sorry. It's what it is, for now. Can you source the camera footage for me please, Stuart?"

"Yeah, I'll get on it right away on one proviso."

"Go on." Katy sensed what was coming next.

"You tell us what happened first."

Katy glanced around the bar and leaned over it. "I'm trusting you with this information. He perished in his car. That's all I'm prepared to say at this point. Please, don't hold back any information that could help us solve this crime; otherwise, I might think you have an ulterior motive."

"Oh, fuck! No, I wouldn't dream of it. Poor Jason. And you think this woman was behind it?" Stuart asked, raking a hand through his greying hair.

"It's a possibility. We won't know what her involvement is until we track her down and have a chat with her. We can't do that without the proof of who she is. Which I'm hoping you'll be able to provide."

Stuart turned his back on them and shouted over his shoulder, "Let me get things lined up for you. I'll give you a shout once I've teed everything up."

Tracey was standing there shaking her head, bulging tears brimming in her blue eyes. "I'm in shock. I can't believe what you're saying. She seemed pretty nice to me. A bit tarty, but nice all the same."

"Can you tell us how they met?"

"Sure, he was sat at one end of the bar and she was at the other. She smiled at him and he wandered down the bar and sat on the stool next to her. He bought her a drink. They were laughing, he's a terrible one for telling awful jokes, most of them are rude… at least he used to be, sorry, forgot myself there. I can't believe he's gone. Sometimes he was a pain in the butt, trying it on with me, I knew he was married though. How's his wife taken the news or is that a dumb question?"

"Both she and her daughter are distraught. Going back to this woman, can you describe her at all?"

"Hmm… let me see. She was a brunette with long hair and her boobs, well, every woman's envy gene would be on full alert there. Huge they were."

"And you're sure you haven't seen her in here before?"

"I never forget a face, I suppose you could say it's essential in my job. A good customer service, recognising people, I mean, keeps the punters coming back to line Stuart's pockets."

"Were they together long?"

"Gosh, I can't say I was clock-watching that much last night because I was kept on my toes most of the time, it was quite busy for a mid-week session. Maybe an hour or so. However, don't quote me on that."

"I see. And they appeared to be getting along all right?"

"Yes. I caught snippets of their conversation and have to say there was a hell of a lot of flirting going on, from both sides, not just from him."

"Did you overhear anything that you think might be useful to our enquiries?"

Tracey's head inclined to one side. "Such as what?"

"Did she mention where she lived, what work she did perhaps?"

Tracey glanced sideways at the optics beside her and then nodded. "Yes, she mentioned she was a model, at least I think she did."

"A model?"

"I caught the tail end of the conversation. Again, don't quote me on this, but I'd say she was one of those underwear models. Let's just say she had the figure for lingerie and leave it there, shall we?"

"See, now that kind of information could be essential to our investigation."

"I hope it is. Jason didn't deserve to die. I know I'm reading between the lines here, but are you saying you think this woman killed him?"

"We have no way of knowing that at this stage. If she was the last person to see him then yes, it would make sense to lay the blame at her door. Which is why it's imperative we find her ASAP."

"I get that. Let me chase Stuart up for you. He's been known to step into his office and get distracted at times." She left the bar area and returned a few seconds later. "As suspected. Why don't you come round? I'll show you through to the office." She motioned for them to join her at the other end of the bar and held open the door for them to enter. Tracey then showed them to the office.

"Come in. I'm nearly there. Why don't you take a seat?"

Katy and Charlie sat opposite him. He angled the monitor so all three of them could see and pressed play. "That's Jason there." He blew out a breath. "I'll miss him. Interesting chap, always had a take on everything under the sun. Made me think mostly that there are different perspectives to all manner of things in this life."

"Sounds like a fascinating character."

"Yeah, he kept his customers entertained, that's for sure, according to what he used to tell me, anyway. I reckon he spent more time chatting than he did working when he showed up at some of his regulars. It's the old ladies, you see, he had them eating out of his hand. Lonely old biddies, always keen on having a man tend to their needs."

Katy frowned at his odd statement. "Are you telling me he used to rip his customers off?"

"Good Lord, no. He wouldn't dream of doing that, not in a million years. He cared about his customers, some more than others; he went the extra mile, offered them more than they paid for... like a few hours of pleasurable company. Damn, here I go again, I'm not very good with words and keep putting my bloody size twelves in it. What I'm trying to say is he cared about people, his customers. Had his head screwed on there. Always said if you lend an ear, the older ladies treat you well and you always get repeat business."

"Makes perfect sense to me. What about the younger ladies on his customer list?"

His mouth drooped down at the sides. "I'm not sure he had any, not that he ever spoke about. Ah, here we are, this is the young woman Tracey was on about. Good grief!" His eyes almost popped out of his head.

Katy glanced at Charlie who appeared to be equally shocked by the woman's appearance on the screen. "Okay, can you fast forward to where he joins her?"

Stuart hit the button, but never took his eyes off the screen, appearing to be mesmerised by the young woman. "Crikey, I can see why Jason felt the urge to talk to her. Sorry, maybe that was uncalled for."

"What's not to like? A pretty, well-endowed woman walks into the room, it stands to reason that men would be drawn to her."

"And some. Bloody hell, it's a good job my wife's not here right now. That's all I can say. I'd be black and blue just for playing the tape."

Katy chuckled. "Your wife wouldn't be a tad insecure, would she?"

He tapped the side of his nose. "Yep, she is that." He froze the screen once Jason had joined the young woman. "Want me to continue?"

"Yes, if you wouldn't mind." Katy withdrew her notebook and jotted down the distinguishing features of the woman, noting any wonkiness in her teeth as she smiled, going above and beyond what she would normally do in such cases, trying to satisfy the feeling she had that this woman might possibly go to ground. "And this is where they get up to leave."

"Yep. I can switch to the outside cameras if you give me a sec."

"Brilliant, thanks."

The camera switched from a bright one to one that was lit by the outside lights and the customer car park. "That's Jason's Pathfinder over there."

They watched the giggling couple hop into the vehicle. Jason, being the gent, opened the door for the woman before he ran around the front of the vehicle to jump behind the steering wheel. Then the car left the area.

"That's great. At least, we can place the woman in his car after they left the pub, always a good sign in an investigation."

"Do you need a copy?"

"That would be excellent. We can't thank you enough. It'll definitely help, having the footage to hand."

He inserted a disc, pressed another button and looked up to ask, "Will you be running one of those appeals on TV?"

"Possibly. We'll see how things pan out first."

With the task completed, he placed the disc back in its case and handed it to Katy. "My pleasure, I'm always happy to help the police whenever I can."

He saw them back through to the bar area. Katy smiled and shook his hand. "It's much appreciated. Let's hope we find the woman concerned, and quickly."

"I hope you bloody bring her to justice when you do. Poor Jason, he shouldn't have gone out that way."

Katy and Charlie left the pub and returned to the cars. Katy placed the disc on the passenger seat beside her. Charlie leaned on the driver's door and looked down at her. "And so it begins. Let's hope we find this bloody woman soon."

"What's her motive?" Charlie asked, her brow furrowed. "Do you think she intentionally went in there to trap a man in her web and do away with him? Or do you reckon Jason was specifically targeted?"

"Both valid questions that I just don't have an answer to, as yet. On the positive side, we have an image of her. If we get desperate, we'll share that with the media, but only as a last resort. I'd rather try and catch her using our detective skills, keep our attempts under the radar for now. The last thing we want to do is give her the heads-up and for her to take off, it's only going to bloody frustrate us in the long run."

"I get that, but where do we start?"

"We need to see if Patti has found any possible DNA at the crime scene."

"Tough one, considering the car was burnt out."

"I know. Let the daunting task of the mammoth mission that lies ahead of us begin. See you back at the station. I'll stop off and pick up something for the gang to eat."

En route back to base, Katy stopped off at the baker's around the corner to buy lunch for the team. They were going to have a long afternoon ahead of them, and it was important for them to keep their strength up; what better way to do that than with a hot pulled pork roll and a sticky iced bun? Sod the calories, needs must at times.

The team were grateful for the sustenance Katy and Charlie appeared with. They were just tucking into their lunch when DCI Roberts decided to pop his head around her office door.

"Caught you at a bad time, have I?"

"A girl has got to eat sometimes. Take a seat, sir, what can I do for you?"

"I was hoping we could have a brief chat about Charlie."

Katy frowned and pushed her lunch aside. She wiped her mouth on a napkin and said, "Something wrong?"

He waved away her suggestion. "Ever the detective. No, nothing is wrong. I wondered how she was doing since her promotion, that's all."

Katy loved seeing him on the ropes. He looked awkward and shifted in his seat. "In what respect? If you're asking me whether the power has gone to her head, then no, it hasn't. Women aren't like that, it's the men who are usually keen to exert their authority, in my experience."

He squirmed some more and winced. "Ouch! I suppose I asked for that. Maybe we should veer off the subject, I'm sensing you're super prickly today."

Katy sniggered. "Only when you raise a daft subject. Tell me, have you spotted a difference in Charlie since she obtained her promotion?"

Sean sat back in his chair, steepled his fingers and rested them against his chin. "No, I can't say I have. Ignore me, I shouldn't have singled her out."

"By that, you mean you haven't done the rounds checking up on how other sergeants who have recently been promoted have adapted to their new roles?"

"Ah, you've caught me out."

Katy refused to let the subject drop, he'd succeeded in getting her back up now, picking on her partner. "Why Charlie? Is it because of who her mother is? I know you two had a history, but come on, Sean, give the girl a break."

He sighed and shook his head. "You're reading more into this than is necessary, Katy, and no, it's not because she is Lorne Simpkins' daughter. It's because I have a genuine interest in her career. I've always predicted that she will go a long way, I aim to keep her on course, if it's possible. Is there something wrong with that?"

"Nope. Why didn't you say that in the first place, instead of going all around the houses to get to your point, Sean?"

He grinned. "That would be because I'm a man and tend to engage my mouth before my brain."

Her tension eroded, and Katy finally broke into a smile. "No disrespect intended, but you're a strange one at times."

He cocked an eyebrow, but his eyes sparkled with merriment. "In your professional opinion, of course."

"Of course."

"Tell me what you're working on?"

"We've spent the morning speaking to the family of a deceased man. He was found early this morning in a burnt-out car. Not pretty, as you can imagine."

"Ouch! Any idea what happened?"

"It was deliberately torched. Patti suspects the man was bound inside his vehicle before it went up in flames."

"So he couldn't have escaped?"

"About sums it up." Katy sighed. "Speaking to the wife and daughter, it turns out he was a bit of a sex pest. I think the wife has led a tormented life over the years; he abused their daughter and was violent towards her."

"Could either of them be guilty of killing him?"

"I don't think so, but I definitely haven't crossed them off the suspect list, not yet. However, when Charlie and I showed up at the pub he frequented *a lot,* the barmaid told us that he got talking to, or should I say he was flirting with, a young woman last night and ended up leaving with her. So she has to be our main suspect."

"Can you ID the woman?"

"We've got CCTV footage of her. Plus, we have proof that he gave her a lift in his car. So that definitely puts her in the frame for being the last person to be seen with him."

"Interesting. Did the barmaid know this woman? Could she put a name to her?"

"Nope. She told me that Jason had an eye for the ladies. Maybe the woman was aware of that and targeted him intentionally."

"As some kind of payback?"

Katy shrugged. "Who knows? In my experience, it's rare to find a killer out on the prowl just for the sake of it."

"Good point. So you think she was against the type of man he was as opposed to him as a person?"

"The honest answer to that is I really don't know." She let out a deep sigh. "That's the huge undertaking we have ahead of us."

"Press conference?"

"Too soon. The last thing I want to do is drive the woman underground."

"You think she's likely to strike again?"

"Your guess is as good as mine on that one."

He rose from his chair. "I'll let you get back to your lunch. Keep me informed."

"Thanks. I'll do that, as and when I can."

He left the office. Katy glanced out of the window at the black clouds up above. She watched the speed they were travelling at, momentarily mesmerised by their intensity and movement. "Hey, this isn't getting any work done, shake a leg, missus!"

She returned to her roll, consumed another third of it and threw the rest in the bin. After downing the remains of her lukewarm coffee, she joined the team in the incident room.

Charlie eyed her with caution. Katy knew what was running through her mind. Her partner was intrigued to know if everything was all right after the chief's visit. She smiled, putting her partner at ease.

"Okay, now lunch is out of the way, let's get down to business." She turned to bring the whiteboard up to date with the name of the victim. "Jason Davis, married to Jane, daughter Sammy. While the wife and daughter were both upset, I sensed there was some form of relief coming from the wife. He abused their daughter when she was ten. Saying that, Sammy idolised her father. Which must have put a strain on the family unit. He spent a minimum of four nights a week at The Fallow Deer Inn. Charlie and I dropped over there and picked up the CCTV footage from last night. It proved that his attention was drawn to a young woman. I don't wish to cast aspersions, but you'll be able to see for yourself what I mean, she's not your run-of-the-mill type of woman out for a drink. In my opinion, she's 'dressed to kill' some might say, pun intended. Stephen, can you run the disc for me?"

He inserted the disc into his computer, and the image appeared on the large screen against the far wall.

"As you can see, they seemed comfortable in each other's company, so much so that after a while, they left the pub together." The image changed to outside. "This is the last picture we have of the couple. They drove out of the car park and turned right in the direction of the piece of wasteland where Jason's body was found, inside his burnt-out vehicle."

"Would it be worth checking the area for any other cameras?" Graham asked.

"If you wouldn't mind doing that, Graham, just so we have the necessary backup for when or if this trial goes to court. Of course, before it gets to that point, we're going to have to catch ourselves a bloody suspect first."

"I'll get on it right away, boss," Graham replied.

"Will it be worth running the woman through the database?" Charlie suggested.

"Definitely, although I have an inkling nothing will show up. I don't mind admitting that I think this one is going to lead us into places we'd rather not tread."

"Meaning?" Charlie inclined her head.

"I can't put my finger on it. Maybe it's far too early to assume what we're up against here, but I have a niggling feeling that the motive is revenge."

"Why?" Charlie asked.

"Intuition and yes, I know I'm not usually a great believer in such trash, but let's face it, what else have we got to go on right now?"

"That's true enough. What do you want us to do?"

"The usual checks. He's self-employed, see what state his business was in. Check if he worked from home or if he had another base. His finances. Any possible loans, take that route into consideration as well."

"Enough for us to be getting on with," Charlie replied. She spun her chair around to face her desk and pounded her keyboard. Katy smiled and left the team to it while she got back to her own paperwork in the office.

Oh, the unambiguous joy of being a detective inspector in the Met.

3

You need to do it, and quickly! Time's a-wasting. You've begun your journey now. Don't neglect your duties.

You have debts to repay. Revenge to seek.

They did it. They ruined your life. It's time to right so many wrongs. You've waited long enough. Don't hold back or take the coward's way out. Don't you dare!

They need to be punished and you're the only person to do it. To avenge their heinous crimes against your loved ones. Go forth and do your stuff.

Megan woke from the nap she'd been having. Her exertions from the previous evening had taken their toll on her body. She wasn't built for this kind of trauma. The desire driving her ambitions had a lot to answer for. It was just gone four in the afternoon, and she was expected at her aunt's house at five. She'd better get a move on, she hated being late.

She showered, dried her long blonde hair and tied it back in a ponytail. It was the only way her brother would recognise her. Tears surfaced and threatened to spill as the memories of their fragile childhood replayed in her mind. She adored her brother, always had done.

Spending as much time with him as possible put her life back into perspective. She was going through all this bother for his benefit, not just hers.

Megan left her flat, traipsed down the stairs and jumped in her car. She drove the mile or so to her aunt and uncle's home. It was far more practical for Daniel to live there, rather than with her. Between them, a long time ago, they had decided it was for the best.

She used the key to let herself in and called out, "Hello, anybody home?"

"It's Megan, Daniel, she's here," her aunt shouted excitedly from the lounge.

"I'm coming. Are you ready for me, Daniel?"

She heard her brother's usual grunting which intensified the second he laid eyes on her. He reached out a gnarled hand, his head tilting in its usual position against the headrest of his chair.

Her heart swelled, it was always the same. Amazed that he recognised her in spite of his disabilities. She rushed forward and hugged him, willing herself not to shed a tear. She hated showing any kind of emotion in front of him; he always picked up on when she was upset.

"Me, Me," he shouted. Sadly, he had a limited vocabulary.

She smiled and stroked his face. "Hello my precious, Daniel. How are you today?"

"Me, Me."

She undid the zip of her bag and extracted a present she'd bought for him. Holding the small gift in front of his face, she tore off the wrapping paper and presented him with the Corgi sports car—it was yellow, his favourite colour. A smile touched his lips. It was a fleeting gesture, and with a tissue, she wiped up the dribble that escaped from his mouth.

"He loves your little gifts, Megan. Come, we'll go through to the kitchen, your uncle is due home soon. I've made a chicken casserole, is that okay for you?"

"Sounds wholesome and divine. You're such a good cook, Auntie Gail, I'm grateful for any meal you lay on for when I come to visit. How has Daniel been this week?"

"You're always welcome at our table. Look at you, you're too skinny, my girl. It's my mission in life to put some excess pounds on those bones of yours. Therefore, we have chocolate gateau for afters."

Megan groaned at the thought of feeding her brother and the mess they'd need to clear up afterwards. But Daniel loved chocolate, so the mess would be worth it. "I bet Daniel can't wait. Did you deliberately avoid my question?"

"No, sorry. My mind is all over the place today. I've had to up his trips to the physio this week, he's been a little stiffer than normal."

"Do you need me to stop over and help out with his care? You know I will, you only have to ask."

"I know, but you have your own life to lead. We're stuck in a routine, we're coping. Every now and again, his muscles either spasm or seize up. He'll be fine soon, don't worry. As long as he's still got a smile on his face every time you walk into the room, that's all that matters, isn't it?"

"I feel so guilty, leaving his care to you and Uncle Sam."

"We've been over this a number of times. We love you both as our own, yes, some days are harder than others, I'm not disputing that, love." Her aunt sighed and then smiled. "It's challenging and rewarding at the same time. We know he loves us, and appreciates everything we do for him. He's a treasure we refuse to give up on. We remember back in the day, when the pair of you used to come and visit us when you were kids."

Megan walked over and hugged her aunt. She drew back and wiped both of their tears. "I can't thank you enough for putting your life on hold for us both. We love you and Uncle Sam so much."

"I made a promise to your mother long before she died that we would look after you both should anything happen."

"I know you did. But at the time, none of us could have known how bad Daniel was going to be, he was in that damn coma for months."

"The memory is still so vivid in my mind. You know Sam and I would go to the end of the world for you two. You're part of us. We love you both to bits. Go, I'll tend to the dinner, you go and sit with Daniel, he hates to be left alone."

"I love you so much, Auntie Gail. Don't ever think I take you for granted because I would never do that."

"I'm aware of that. Shoo… out of my kitchen; otherwise, you'll have me spilling my tears in the casserole and we can't have that, can we?"

Megan hugged her aunt again and returned to the lounge. She sat next to her brother, running the small car across his legs and up his arms, making him groan in delight. She mopped up his dribble again and kissed him on the forehead. Squeezing him lightly, she whispered, "Revenge will be ours soon, sweetie. You might not be aware of what's going on, but I will never forget what those fuckers did to you… to our parents. I love you so much."

"It's always wonderful to see you two together, Megan."

She spun around, surprised to see her uncle standing there, beaming at her. *Shit! Had he overheard what she'd said to Daniel?* Judging by the loving expression on his chubby face, she didn't think so.

Megan met her uncle in the middle of the room, and they hugged tightly and kissed each other on the cheek. "How are you, Uncle Sam?"

"Oh, you know, could be better, but there again I could be worse. We muddle through, don't we?"

"You know you only need to ring me if you need help with Daniel, don't you?"

"Yes. Except I wasn't talking about your brother, I was talking about work. They told me today that they were," he glanced back at the kitchen door and whispered the rest of his sentence, "cutting my hours in half."

Megan gasped. "Bloody hell. How will you cope?"

"That's not your concern, love. We'll cope, even if we have to apply for extra benefits, we'll make sure we cope. On the bright side, it'll allow me to spend more time with my pal here." He went over to

Daniel and fist bumped him. "Hey, Daniel, we'll have fun spending more time together."

With that, Gail came back into the room. "Oh, Lord, what are you planning now? The last excursion we took to feed the ducks ended up with you fishing Daniel out of the lake."

"What?" Megan said, horrified.

Her uncle slung his arm around Megan's shoulders and tutted. "Don't listen to her. There was a slope, I took a picture with my camera and forgot to apply the brake on Daniel's chair. He rolled down the hill and into the edge of the water. He loved it, wouldn't stop laughing." He pinched Daniel's cheek. "Didn't you, mate? Being up close and personal with the ducks."

Daniel shared a special smile with them. "Me, Me, duck!"

They all laughed. Megan mopped up the dribble again as if it were second nature. "Maybe we can all go to the park soon and feed the ducks? It's been a while since I did anything as exciting as that."

"We'll see. Right. Go wash your hands, you, horrible lot. Dinner will be ready in five minutes," Gail ordered.

Uncle Sam raced out of the room and up the stairs to get changed, while Megan wheeled her brother into his specially adapted bathroom in the downstairs extension the council had recently funded. It had everything installed to make Daniel's life easier. There was a hoist on a rail that led into the box-shaped shower room, so Auntie Gail was able to place Daniel in the hoist and easily transport him to take a shower every morning. She'd told Megan that lately, Daniel's personal hygiene had intensified as he seemed to soil himself more and more during the day.

It was an anxious time for all of them, caring for Daniel. Although the lion's share fell on her aunt's and uncle's shoulders, she made sure to help when she could.

She wheeled him up to the sink, ran the hot water and added just enough cold to lower the temperature to tepid. She dipped his blue flannel in the water and smothered it in soap. His head juddered from side to side, anticipating what she was about to do. "Now sit still, wriggler."

"Me, Me, ducks!"

"She laughed. You are funny. I'm not going to wet you that much, just enough to clean you up. Don't you want your dinner, Daniel?"

"Me, Me, ducks!"

"I'll take you to see the ducks at the weekend, I promise, all right? Now, be good and stay still for Megan."

"Me, Me, love you."

Her heart swelled with joy and love. Her brother truly was the sweetest person she knew. His life had imploded the night of the accident, and now this was what they all had to contend with. While none of them complained about caring full-time for him, there were times when she wished she had her old brother back. The brother she used to go on adventure holidays with, who she loved nothing more than to embark on rock-climbing and windsurfing expeditions with. All that was a distant memory for both of them now, if Daniel even remembered those times.

After cleaning his face and hands and drying them thoroughly, she wheeled him back through the house and into the kitchen. He sat at the head of the oblong table with Megan on one side of him and Auntie Gail on the other. They took it in turn to feed him while trying to feed themselves at the same time. It was a routine they'd come up with a long time ago; it allowed everyone to enjoy their meals while they were still hot, and all four of them ate together instead of enduring staggered sittings. They were a unit, each of them having a role to play in caring for Daniel so his life was as normal as they could make it.

Her brother turned his head away from Auntie Gail. "Me, Me, do it."

"No, Daniel, it's Auntie's turn. Be a good boy now."

"Me, Me." He banged his fist on the arm of his chair.

A hurt expression flashed across her aunt's face. Megan's sympathy gene notched up. It was hard for her aunt to take rejection. "It's okay, love. You feed him. I might get to eat a hot dinner for a change, eh?" Her aunt winked at her, keeping her tone light and jolly.

Megan mouthed an apology and fed Daniel in between eating small mouthfuls of her own dinner, which was delicious as usual. Auntie Gail was one of the best cooks she knew. It was always a pleasure to come here for a meal; at least, she was guaranteed to get something other than a bowl of cereals or beans on toast.

She fed Daniel until he'd had enough and refused to open his mouth, then she concentrated on eating the rest of her meal. Her aunt and uncle were easy to talk to, they spoke about what each of their day's had consisted of and always involved Megan in the conversation.

"When is your next day off, dear?" Auntie Gail asked.

Although Megan had booked a few days off in order to carry out her audacious plan, she had no intention of telling her family. "Not until next Wednesday. I'm having to work extra shifts at the moment as there are several colleagues off work, either through holidays or sickness. I don't mind though, more money for me, right?"

"You work too hard. A young lady of your age should be out there enjoying herself," her uncle admonished good-naturedly.

"You worry too much. I adore my life. Maybe *adore* is a tad over the top, I love it, how's that? Gone are the days where I go out clubbing every night, not that I ever did that, not really. I'm too much of a home girl, you know that." She glanced at her brother whose eyelids were drooping. "I miss spending time with Daniel and the adventure sports we used to throw ourselves into as kids."

"It needn't be like that, not nowadays," her uncle said. He left the table and returned to place a brochure down beside her.

She opened it and flicked through the pages. "My goodness, how on earth did you hear about this?"

He tapped his nose. "I have a few contacts. What do you think? Daniel would love to do something like that, wouldn't he?"

Megan angled the brochure in her brother's direction. "What do you think, Daniel? Would you like to go to an adventure park one day?"

His eyes drooped even more until a soft snore escaped.

"Maybe not." Her uncle laughed.

"We'll ask him again when he's less sleepy. I'll need to do some research into the facility, but it looks to be a thrilling experience for both abled and disabled alike. It would be wonderful to go with him, I'm sure he'd be delighted at the chance to do it." She smiled at the man who had cared for her, treating her as his own daughter, since she was very young. "Thanks, Uncle Sam, you're the best. You both are. I don't have a clue what our lives would be like if you hadn't stepped up to the plate and offered your home to care for him. We're both so appreciative of you putting your lives on hold to ensure he has a quality of life like no other." Her eyes misted up and she dabbed at them with her serviette.

"Hush now, you'll start me off," Auntie Gail said, swiping a serviette across her eyes. "It's a pleasure. Our lives have been enriched immeasurably by having you two around us. We don't see caring for Daniel as a hardship, we see it as a calling. It's made better people out of the pair of us, in the long run."

"You've sacrificed so much over the years to take care of us. I just want you to know that both Daniel and I love you for putting your lives on hold to make ours more fulfilling."

Her uncle squeezed her hand and smiled. "Megan, it's what families do for each other. Your parents were both very special people, it broke our hearts the day they died eighteen years ago. Gosh, has it really been that long? I guess it must be. The time has flown by, you know why?"

"No. Why?" she asked.

"Because we've enjoyed every single minute of it. You mustn't think looking after Daniel is a chore for us. No doubt there are days where we think that, but as a rule, we do it because we want to and not because we *have* to."

"Words fail me as usual. You were not obliged to step into our parents' shoes, but you did it without a second thought. In my opinion, that shows how much compassion you have running through your souls. I'll always be grateful to you, especially with the anniversary coming up."

"Anniversary?" Auntie Gail frowned and looked over at her husband.

"Of the crash," Uncle Sam filled in.

"Oh my! How silly of me. You really shouldn't dwell on that, Megan. Try to ignore the date when it comes around every year. We can do little about it, it's not as if we can turn back the clock, is it? As much as we'd all want to do that, it's time we forgot about the past and lived for the future."

Megan smiled and reached out for her aunt's and uncle's hands. "As I've said a thousand times before, you're both angels in this world in which there are so many dark demons. It's a better place with you in it, of that I'm certain."

"Count yourself in that equation too, Megan, you're a very special young woman who deserves nothing but the best in this life. The way you put your brother's needs before your own... not every twenty-something would be willing to do that."

"Daniel and you guys are all I have left. I intend to share every spare moment I can with you."

"And we with you. The offer is always there for you to move in permanently," Auntie Gail stated for the umpteenth time.

Although Megan was severely tempted to accept the offer this time around, there was something stopping her. Maybe she'd be more willing to accept their kind offer once she'd rid herself of the angst building up inside, fuelling her need to right the wrongs of a distant past that had shaped both her brother's and her own life over the years. "Let me mull it over. All I know is that I miss you guys when I'm not here, but something is stopping me from taking the plunge."

"Oh, what's that?" Uncle Sam asked.

"The last thing I want is for you to feel pressured into sharing your home with me. On the flip side, at my age, I should be craving my independence."

"But you're not. I can tell you're wavering. Coming around to our way of thinking. No pressure from us, love, you take your time. Weigh up the pros and cons and let us know what you decide. Right, who's for dessert?"

"Sounds like a good idea. What's on the menu?"

"Chocolate gateau."

Megan groaned. "Oh my, ten thousand calories, here we come. If I did succumb and move in, I fear I'd be thirty stone before long."

Auntie Gail stood while her husband gathered the plates. "Get away with you."

The couple left her to be with her brother who was still dozing in his wheelchair. She mulled over their suggestion again. Tempted to finally give in to their wishes. She nodded, silently agreeing to put her notice in on her flat at the end of the following month when her rent was due. But first, she had a daunting mission ahead of her. She would need to take her time. It had taken her months to locate the men and she'd had them under surveillance during the evenings for the past few weeks. It had been an eye-opener for her as each of the different elements of her plan had formed. Her intentions were to hit them all swiftly, within a few days of each other so none of them cottoned on to what was happening and warned the others.

The second hit was due to take place that evening, once she'd said farewell to her family. She had to time her departure correctly. If she left too soon, there was a danger someone might spot her hanging around while she waited for her next victim to leave work. She smiled at the thought of killing another of her enemies, part of the gang who...

"Here we go. Shall we wake Daniel up or do you think he should sleep a little longer?" her aunt asked. She placed a large portion of gateau in front of Megan.

"Crikey, that's huge. I'm not sure I have enough room for that amount."

"Get away with you, it'll do you good to have some wholesome food in that tiny stomach of yours."

Megan shook her head and suggested, "Why don't we leave Daniel for now? He might wake up once he hears us eating."

Two hours later, it was time for Megan to make a move, despite her aunt pleading with her to stay the night. She kissed her sleepy brother goodbye.

"Bye, Me, Me."

"I'll see you at the weekend, sweetheart. Be good until then, okay?"

"Good, Me, Me."

She circled her finger around his cheek, something he always appreciated, and made him smile.

Her aunt hugged her and remained with Daniel. Uncle Sam saw her out to her car. He squeezed her tightly. "Think about what we said, no pressure either way, love."

"Thank you. I'll consider it, I promise."

He stepped back to allow her to get in the car and remained by the gate, waving goodbye until she turned the next corner on her way into town. She felt blessed to have such a compassionate couple in her life.

She eased through the traffic, aware she had ten minute's grace to get to the store before closing time.

The orange sign drew her towards it like a beacon. Megan parked her car next to another and then realised her mistake—it might belong to a member of staff. Consequently, she moved to the centre and switched off her engine. Hunkered down in her seat, she watched and waited, grateful that it was already dark at this hour, although the clocks were due to go forward in a few weeks, which would alter things considerably.

The staff left the rear of the building, a few at a time. As each group appeared, her heart lurched a little. Finally, Bobby Simmonds appeared. Dressed head to foot in Lycra, he wheeled his bike out of the building and locked up behind him. He punched in the number for the alarm and mounted his bike.

Megan waited until he cycled past and then started her engine. She kept a gap between them and followed him into the traffic which had calmed down considerably since her arrival. Bobby cycled hard and fast. He was a fitness freak, who liked to push himself whenever and wherever possible. It was a ten-mile trek out to his house. He accelerated and slowed down regularly during his journey, blissfully unaware that he was being followed.

Megan bided her time before making her move. The spot she'd

chosen was a couple of miles away now. All she needed to do was to keep a safe distance behind him, for now.

Bobby sped up again. This time his stint at pushing himself was extended. Before long, they'd reached the spot Megan had selected. His tempo slowed once more, and Megan prepared herself for the attack. Squeezing her foot down on the accelerator, she moved right up behind him.

He motioned for her to overtake. She had no intention of doing as he suggested. She revved the engine and the car surged forward, she braked and then dropped back. He glanced over his shoulder, an angry expression chiselled into his features. He was shouting at her, urging her to go past him.

Again, she slammed her foot down hard and propelled forward. She hit the rear wheel, the bike swerved violently and ended up rebounding out of the hedge. Megan glanced in her rear-view mirror, pressed her foot on the brake and reversed at speed. The car bounced over the bike and Bobby. She paused to see if there was any movement from him. Peering through the windscreen, she saw his fingers move.

"Die, you bastard, die!"

She thrust the gear stick into first and drove forward a second time. The car humped over the obstruction. Another glance in the mirror and all was still this time. Just to make sure, she drove backwards and forwards another five times. *Overkill? Maybe, but it'll be worth it. He shouldn't have been involved in their deaths. Revenge will be mine.*

Two down, another two to go.

She continued down the country lane to the next village and turned right. The road led back into town. Her adrenaline was pumping fast. That was two men she'd killed in the last twenty-four hours; she should at least feel some form of remorse, shouldn't she? Instead, she was buzzing, the thrill of the kill seeping into her nerve endings. *I could get used to this! Do I want to get used to it? That's the question!*

She didn't, that was the answer, pure and simple. She said it over and over again. *Once the plan is complete, I'll hang up my killing gloves and get on with my life.* She repeated the mantra several times as if trying to convince herself.

A niggling doubt crept in for the tiniest of moments. *What if they catch me? What will happen to Daniel then? How will he cope without me?*

However, the doubts weren't strong enough for her to reconsider her plan. As far as she was concerned, these men deserved to die and she would see to it they suffered in their deaths, too, just like her parents had.

4

"Oh, what a joy! Another weekend shift to look forward to. What have we ever done that was so wrong to be dealt this hand?" Katy complained. They were en route to yet another crime scene.

Charlie groaned. "Maybe someone up there is trying to tell us something."

"Perhaps you're right. All I know is that I was enjoying my morning cuddle with AJ a little too much this morning, in fact, between you and me, I almost picked up the phone and rang in sick."

Her partner shot her a sideways glance and gasped. "You would never do that. You're far too professional to sink to that level, aren't you?"

"Yeah, you know me too well. It's just, some mornings, especially when you have a sexy, hot blooded male in your bed, it's more difficult to leave than others."

Sniggering, Charlie said, "Crikey, I bet AJ would be all of a dither if he ever heard you talk about him in that way."

Katy cringed and conceded, "You're probably right. Hey, I'm still classed as a newlywed, so maybe it's acceptable, for now. Enough about me. You haven't raised the subject lately, and I haven't felt inclined to push you on the matter, but how has Brandon been since your promotion? The last I heard, he was giving you some grief."

"One day he's as good as gold and the next he doesn't even bother speaking to me. I don't understand it. We used to be so close, you know, before, when I lived at home with Mum and Tony."

"By the sounds of it, you're saying that since you started living together, he's changed."

"Either he has, or dare I say it, I have. Heck, if I have, I haven't noticed."

Katy cast her a quick glance before averting her gaze back to the road ahead. "I doubt if you would. Want my opinion, for what it's worth?"

"Here we go. Go on then, you might as well let me have it, now we're on the subject."

"Don't say it like that. If you'd rather I keep my mouth shut, I will."

"No. Go on. Let me have your valuable insight." There was no sarcasm in Charlie's words and she chuckled.

"You're guilty of growing up, and maybe he's yet to catch up. Every day, I notice a change in you. You're becoming far more confident. Now, whether the change has been down to your recent promotion, I don't think it is."

Charlie fell quiet and glanced out of the side window. She watched the fields passing by for a moment and then turned her way. "I haven't really thought about it. Working with you has definitely brought me out of my shell. If that means I've grown in confidence, I'm not so sure."

"I am, because it's true. I've seen it happen so many times over the years. Not just in this job, but amongst my friends who had big ambitions. Their partners, most of the time, took umbrage at their success."

"Really? Maybe it's a male ego problem, although I couldn't aim that at Brandon, he's so inoffensive, most of the time."

The traffic came to a standstill and Katy drummed her fingers on the steering wheel. "He's a sweetheart, from what I've seen of him. But men are strange creatures, maybe that's why AJ felt the need to start up his new business in the end. Who knows what's going on in their heads, unless they come right out and tell you?"

"You two have a fabulous relationship. Not every man would have put his career on hold and chosen to be a househusband." Charlie lowered the window to rid the car of the stuffiness that had descended.

The car behind beeped, startling Katy into action. She slotted into gear and pulled away. "I know. I'm indebted to him for being a super dad and caring for Georgie so well. I could never stand in his way in the future, I will always be conscious of the sacrifices he made for our family. Sorry, I didn't mean to turn the conversation to me, that wasn't my intention."

"You didn't, at least, I didn't take it that way. Maybe the situation has highlighted a flaw in our relationship that I hadn't realised was there. I adore my job, yes, I might complain about it now and again, but on the whole, I find it exhilarating. To go home every night and not be able to share how my day went with him is extremely hard."

"Wait, why can't you do that, within reason of course?"

"Because he just stares at me as though either I've lost him or he's plainly not interested in what I'm telling him."

"Ouch! That's not very nice. Not casting aspersions on Brandon or anything, but I reckon he needs a good shake-up. Any man who loves his woman should find her interesting, whether she's stuck at home looking after the children, baking all day long, or the opposite, at work, and in our case, putting our lives on the line every day. Maybe you're going to need to sit him down and thrash out what he expects from your relationship."

"Looking back, I think his attitude changed when I joined the K9 team," Charlie admitted after a few minutes of silence.

"He's always worked with dogs, hasn't he? Perhaps he might have been a touch envious or jealous of your achievements in that department then, is that what you're saying?"

Charlie sighed. "This is the first time I've really sat down and considered what's wrong. It's hard to tell what's happened. Maybe I need to take the bull by the horns and thrash it out with him."

"I would. It could go two ways, either pull you back together or break you apart. It's got to be worth a try, you can't go on living the way you are, hon. Everyone deserves to be happy in their life. Hey, think about what your parents went through during your childhood, do you really want to go down the same route?"

Charlie raised a pointed finger. "Now you're making me see sense. I always said that I would avoid emulating my parents at all costs. I've been an idiot, I should have had it out with him sooner. Thanks for helping me see the light, Katy."

"Hey, just bear in mind that we're old friends and not just colleagues. Umm… let me correct that, I'm old friends with your mother, but well, I'm always here if you need to bounce ideas off me, Charlie. Sometimes, we're too involved and need to take a step back to see things from an outsider's point of view."

"I hear you. I'm grateful you're not a self-absorbed tyrant of a boss, that's really working in my favour."

"Thanks, I think. We're almost at the location now. I wonder what we'll find this time."

"This is right out in the middle of nowhere, I hope it's not too gruesome, whatever it is."

"I'm with you on that one. I'll let you into a secret."

"What's that?"

"I detest attending a scene first thing in the morning, it's not good on the stomach."

Charlie laughed.

Katy saw the Scene of Crimes vehicles blocking the road up ahead and parked behind the final van. She and Charlie togged up and then headed into the melee. They found Patti crouched next to the victim, talking into her phone and describing the scene on a recording app. She glanced up and stood.

"Hello, you two. No rest for the wicked, eh? Had I known you were on duty over the weekend, I would have rung you direct."

"Thought I'd keep quiet about it just in case you felt the urge to ring me at a godawful hour of the morning. It has been known in the past, Patti." Katy grinned broadly at her pathologist friend.

"Touché, I suppose you're right. Anyway, it's nice to see you both so soon after our last encounter, and don't ask, I haven't got around to doing the PM on that victim yet."

"Too charred or what?"

"No, I simply haven't had the time. I had a two-car pile-up to deal with yesterday afternoon."

"Sorry to hear that. Many deaths?"

"Three, let's just say that kept me busy most of the day. I didn't get home until midnight, then I got the call to attend the scene at seven this morning and well, here I am." She spread her arms wide and slapped them against her thighs.

"So, what have we got? Apart from the obvious, before you fling that one at me."

Patti bared her teeth and then pointed at the victim. "Poor man was run over, several times."

"Several times, as in different cars or the same one?"

"My initial assessment, judging by the tread marks on his body, would be by the same vehicle."

"Bloody hell." Katy surveyed the area. "We're out in the sticks, do you think he was intentionally targeted?"

Patti shrugged. "Your guess is as good as mine. Maybe someone accidentally knocked him off his bike and decided to drive back and forth over him to ensure he was dead, rather than suffer the consequences of being hauled in for dangerous driving."

"That's some imagination you've got there, Patti," Katy replied, dumbfounded by her suggestion.

Patti raised her eyebrows. "Tell me I'm wrong. You can't. Therefore, until we know what went down, that's my input right there. Do with it what you will."

"All right, there's no need for you to get snarky."

"I'm not. It's the only explanation I can muster that has any legs, at this time."

Katy winced and stared at the bone which had broken through the victim's Lycra leggings. "That was terrible, just saying."

Patti smiled. "I know, sorry. I did find his ID in his rucksack. I've placed it in an evidence bag over there."

"Charlie, can you get that for me?" Katy asked, seeing that her partner was standing the closest to the area Patti had indicated.

"His name is Bobby Simmonds. I've got an address. It's on this road, only a few more miles."

"Great news. Who found the body, Patti, do we know?"

"Yes, the man was still here when we arrived. He was shaken up, so I told him to head home. He was with his wife and children, sorry, I should have said that first. They were going to the swimming pool. I think they turned round in the end. Now, where did I put his name and number?" Patti dug into her jacket pocket beneath her protective suit and withdrew a piece of paper. Which turned out to be an old envelope. "Excuse the mess, it was all I had on me and he was eager to get going. Trevor Wardley. To be honest, I doubt if he's going to be able to give you any further details. He rang nine-nine-nine, the control told him to remain here, your lot showed up, taped off the area, called me and bingo bango. I arrived, took down his details and sent him on his way."

"As simple as that, eh? Okay, I'll chase it up once we've had a word with the victim's next of kin. I suppose we should make a move and get that over with just in case they're missing him and set off to find out where he is." Katy searched ahead of them. "I take it the route is blocked?"

"Yep, I've been informed if you go back the way you came, there's a lane on the right about a mile down the road, it circles us and joins the main road at the end."

"Thanks. Is there anything else you can give us before we go?"

"Not really, no. Another point I'd like to make is he was dressed as if he's an experienced cyclist. In my opinion, they don't tend to take any risks, not on roads such as this. That might be worth bearing in mind as well."

"I'll do that. It's looking more and more like an intentional act, isn't it?" Katy nodded thoughtfully.

"Yep, although it might be better to keep an open mind until I've performed the PM."

"We'll be off then. Have you jotted down the address, Charlie?"

"I have. I'll just put the evidence bag back."

Katy said farewell to Patti and walked to the cordoned off perimeter where she deposited her paper suit in the awaiting black bag. Charlie joined her and did the same.

"Now, for the part we hate the most: telling the relatives. I'll ring the witness en route, see if he's up to speaking to us."

They slipped into the car and Katy dialled Trevor Wardley's number.

"Hello, who is this?"

"Hello, Mr Wardley, sorry to disturb you. I'm DI Katy Foster. I'm the Senior Investigating Officer on the crime that was committed this morning. The cyclist being knocked off his bike."

"Ah, yes. Okay. Terrible thing to discover first thing in the morning. My wife and children are still very upset by what they saw."

"I can imagine. Maybe you can run through how you discovered the victim for me."

"I'd rather not, not over the phone. I suppose you'll be needing a statement from me, would it be all right if we left it a few days? Not sure my head is in the right place to consider all the details and I'd hate to miss anything out."

"As you like. Is there that much to tell, sir? Perhaps you can tell me if you saw anyone else in the vicinity? Either on foot or in a vehicle?"

"No, nothing at all. Wait, you might as well hear what I have to say. Let me take the phone in another room."

"Thank you." Katy put the phone on speaker and started the engine. She reversed and trundled down the road taking a right into the lane Patti had mentioned.

"I'm back. Sorry, my kids and wife are really upset, revisiting the incident with them in the room would have brought on another bout of tears."

"No need to apologise. I totally understand. Can I ask what time you stumbled across the victim?"

"Around ten-to-seven, I believe it was. We were on our way for an early morning swim. The pool opens at seven-thirty on a Saturday for special swimming lessons for kids under the age of eleven. We always go then, so my two can have the freedom to learn without other swimmers cursing them for getting in the way."

"I see. Going back to the incident, sir... You found the man lying in the road, did you touch him at all? We need to know for DNA purposes."

"Oh my. Yes, my wife told me off, but by then, it was too late. I felt for a pulse in his neck. I'm sure anyone else in my position would have done the same."

"I have no doubt that's correct. Did you recognise the victim?"

"No. I don't think so. Although, it was hard to tell with the muddy tyre marks covering his face. How could anyone drive over another person like that? I find it utterly barbaric, don't you?"

"Absolutely, I do, that's why we're going to do our very best to punish the person guilty of this atrocious crime."

"How do you propose doing that? There can't be any cameras out on that road."

"We have ways of finding suspects when they least expect it, don't you worry. Of course, at this time, we're reliant on what the witnesses tell us."

"I've failed you then because I really can't tell you much at all."

"It's fine. Please don't be concerned about it. I will need a statement from you, would that be okay?"

"Of course. I'll do anything I can to help the police. When?"

"I'll get in touch with the station, they'll contact you to make the necessary arrangements and take a DNA sample from you."

"Good. Good. Okay, is that all for now?"

"It is. Thank you for speaking with me. Take care of your family and try to put the incident out of your minds if at all possible."

"I'll try. We've got a few videos lined up for the day. A bit of Disney will do the trick, I'm sure."

She smiled. "It always works in my house with my little girl. Thank you again."

"Goodbye. Oh, and I hope you manage to find the person."

"We're going to do our best."

She ended the call and breathed out a sigh. "I had a feeling it was going to be a waste of time. Whoever did this obviously chose the location on purpose, to avoid witnesses, what do you reckon?"

"I think you're right, although that doesn't really help us," Charlie admitted.

"Which is why we're on the way to his home. Hopefully, the victim's wife or girlfriend, assuming he has either, will be able to fill in some of the blanks for us."

She steered the car, narrowly missing a large pothole then pressed her foot on the accelerator and darted down two more roads until they were sitting outside Bobby Simmonds' semi-detached house. The garden was filled with the green shoots of spring, unopened daffodil heads dancing in the slight breeze.

The concrete path had seen better days and they had to pick their way carefully up, for fear they'd catch their heels in larger than average gaps in some sections.

After tackling the obstacle course of the path, Katy rang the doorbell and waited.

A petite woman in her early forties opened the door slightly and poked her head around it. "Yes? What do you want?"

Katy and Charlie produced their IDs. "DI Katy Foster and DS Charlie Simpkins. Are you Mrs Simmonds?"

"For now. What's this about?"

"Would you mind letting us in to discuss the matter?"

"If I must. You'll have to make it snappy, I've arranged to meet my friend in town to go on a shopping trip, what with Easter just around the corner and us having to miss out on Christmas last year."

"It was unfortunate, Christmas being cancelled for everyone, unprecedented times."

She showed them into a neat lounge, which could be described as minimalistic. The only furniture present were two leather sofas, an oak coffee table and a TV stand with a ginormous telly sitting on top of it. "Take a seat."

"Thanks." Katy and Charlie sat opposite the woman. Charlie extracted her notebook and flipped it open. Katy began, "We're here to tell you some bad news."

Mrs Simmonds' hand flew up to cover her mouth. "What? Oh, no, it's not my father, is it? I've told him he should have given up his car years ago. It's too dangerous for him to still be on the road. He went through a red light when we visited Wisbech together last year. My heart was in my mouth at the time."

Katy raised a hand to stop the woman. "No, this has nothing to do with your father and everything to do with your husband."

"Oh, him. What about him?"

"I take it you're not getting along too well at present. You mentioned you were his wife 'for now' at the front door, does that mean you're in the process of getting a divorce?"

"Yes, we're just waiting on the decree absolute to come through; we were promised it would be here at the end of last week, they lied to us. I'm desperate to seek my freedom. I'm done with that man. Can't stand to be in the same room as him now."

Katy nodded. "I understand. Have you been together long?"

"Ten long years. I would have got less time if I'd committed a bad crime, I suspect. Anyway, I've ranted on long enough about that prat, what is it you want to tell me?"

"Unfortunately, your husband's body was found earlier this morning."

"Body? You're not making any sense. What do you...? Oh, God, you're not telling me he's dead, are you?"

"Yes, that's exactly what I'm saying."

Her jaw slackened and her mouth dropped open as she stared at Katy. Her eyes welled up, and she shook her head in disbelief. "I can't believe what you're telling me. Where? How did it happen?"

"A few miles away. He was cycling. Can you tell me what his movements were yesterday?"

"I don't understand."

"He was on his bike, had he gone out for a ride at a particular time?"

"No. I don't think so." She wiped away the tears. "He would have been at work until around eight-ten, eight-fifteen. He locks up the store, you see. Oh, shit, does this mean I'll have to break the news to his mother? She hates me."

"No, we can send someone to do that. Where did Bobby work?" Katy decided to no longer refer to the victim as her husband, due to their circumstances.

"He's, I mean, he was the warehouse manager at B&Q. Bobby was also a fitness freak, he cycled the ten miles or so into work every day. Is that what happened? He was cycling home and had an accident?"

"Possibly. His body was found on the road, close to the bike, so we can't rule it out. I have to ask if you reported him missing last night."

"No. I was out. I stopped over at a friend's house. I got back this morning around nine. I didn't think to check if he'd been home last night or not. He's his own person, so am I. The lockdown last year revealed our marriage wasn't as strong as we thought it was. Hence our decision to part ways."

"I see. Do either of you have different partners, or significant others now?"

"No. We decided it would be better if we respected each other and waited until the divorce came through."

"And yet you're coming across as though you were sick of the sight of him," Charlie added.

She sighed. "I was. We might have agreed for the split to be amicable, but just lately he's pissed me off. Sorry, I know I shouldn't speak ill of the dead. You know when you go down one route and someone tries everything they can to drive you in another direction? Well, that sums up our life. We've been fighting about the proceeds of the house in the past few weeks. He wanted to keep the house, I told him I wanted two hundred grand and the house could be his. He argued it wasn't worth that much and the estate agent more or less agreed. We've been at each other's throats for a couple of weeks over that. Nothing had been sorted and now... now he's dead."

Hmm... could she be responsible for his death in order to gain financially? "And you say you were at a friend's last night?"

Mrs Simmonds nodded.

"We'll need to speak to your friend to verify your account."

The woman's gaze darted between Katy and Charlie. She gasped and shouted, "No! You don't think I could be capable of doing this?"

"No, that's not what I said, Mrs Simmonds. As with any facts, such as an alibi, that surface during an investigation, we need to check them, ensure their accuracy."

"Okay, but why am I getting the impression that I'm a suspect here?"

Guilty conscience perhaps? Katy offered a smile. "I don't know, is there any reason for us to believe you had anything to do with your soon to be ex-husband's accident?"

"No, absolutely *not*. I can't believe you would think such a thing. Bloody hell, I had nothing to do with this." Her voice became high-pitched as she protested her innocence.

"Okay, let's leave that there for now. We'll still need your friend's name and address."

Mrs Simmonds surveyed the room and then rose from her seat to collect her handbag from the corner. She returned, withdrew her phone and scrolled through her contacts. "Jenna Brown, fifty-eight Cheshire Drive. Will that do?" She also gave them Jenna's phone number as well.

"Thanks. We'll get in touch with Jenna later. Going back to Bobby, were you still speaking to each other?"

"Off and on. That doesn't mean that I would set out to hurt him. I'm horrified you should suggest I would."

"I don't recall ever suggesting that, Mrs Simmonds. What I'm trying to ascertain is whether your husb… Bobby mentioned that he'd fallen out with anyone recently."

She contemplated this for a second or two. "No, not that he told me about. Look, what are you saying? This wasn't an accident? Is that why it sounds like you're accusing me of something I wouldn't do? Is that what you're getting at, if I didn't do it, which I didn't, then someone else is responsible?"

"I'm going to lay it on the line for you. The pathologist believes your husband died in suspicious circumstances, and I'm inclined to think along the same lines. Therefore, it's imperative for us to find out what was going on in Bobby's life in the past few weeks and that if something he'd been involved in might have led to him losing his life. That's not to say I'm accusing you of anything, I'm not."

"Well, it bloody sounds like you are to me. And no, Bobby didn't confide in me, not recently. Not ever, really. He was a very secretive individual. Drove me to distraction most of the time. Our marriage had always been a one-sided affair, in my eyes anyway. We rarely shared what we wanted out of life. Initially, I thought he was just shy and a bit reserved and hoped he would come out of his shell once he got to know me better, that never happened."

"I'm sorry to hear that. You hinted at him possibly having a secret, any idea about what?"

"If I knew that, it wouldn't be a secret, would it? I didn't actually say that, I told you he was secretive, in general. Not really about one thing in particular. I know I'm not making any sense, I'm sorry. I know what I want to say, but I don't think I'm expressing myself very well."

"It's a tough situation to get your head around, I completely understand."

"I'm glad you're being reasonable. Take my word for it, as much as I hated Bobby, come the end, I would never dream of hurting him physically. Blimey, have you seen the size of me compared to him?"

"Okay, I think we're done here. I'm going to leave you my card, if you should think of anything you might wish to add, call me."

"And that's it? You're going? What about his parents, are you going to visit them now?"

"If you'll be kind enough to give us their details, yes, we'll go and visit them next. Maybe you can tell me if they've got any underlying health problems we should be aware of?"

"His father has a heart problem and diabetes, other than that, they're both in good health."

"Thanks, that helps a lot." Katy and Charlie stood and Mrs Simmonds showed them to the front door.

"I'm sorry he's dead. You have to believe me. I would never set out to hurt him, not when we'd agreed to go our separate ways."

"We'll be in touch soon, if we find anything out."

She closed the door behind them, and Katy and Charlie walked back to the car.

"What did you make of her?" Katy asked. She wanted to compare Charlie's idea of the woman to her own.

"I'm not sure. To me, her reactions seemed a little false, or was that me reading something into it that simply wasn't there?"

"No, I agree with you. Putting myself in her shoes, I totally get her reaction. Maybe I came across too aggressive back there."

They got in the car and Charlie continued the conversation. "That's nuts! You did not. If you didn't probe, then you wouldn't receive the answers needed to crack the case, would you?"

"There is that. Okay, I'll drive to the parents' house, can't say I'm looking forward to sharing the news with them. Can you call Jenna for me, see if Mrs Simmonds' story is true?"

"We didn't get her first name, did we? Makes it a little awkward."

"Yeah, do your best."

Katy listened to Charlie's end of the conversation. Her partner handled the enquiry well and Jenna furnished her with the facts that Anne Simmonds stayed at Jenna's house and didn't return home until nine that morning.

Katy drummed her fingers on the steering wheel as she drove. "If she didn't do it, then who did? We need to visit the parents first and then head over to B&Q. Maybe someone there can tell us something of use."

The Simmonds' seniors lived in a large bungalow at the end of a quiet cul-de-sac, not far from their son's house. It had a few raised beds in one corner of the front garden, which appeared to have just been planted.

"Can't say I'm looking forward to this," Katy mumbled and rang the bell.

A few moments later, a grey-haired gentleman, sporting a goatee beard and a moustache, opened the door. "Hello? If this is about one of those charities, you're wasting your time. My wife and I only give to reputable dog charities, they need the funds more, in our opinion."

"It's not, Mr Simmonds." Katy flashed her ID. "I'm DI Katy Foster and this is my partner, DS Charlie Simpkins. Would it be all right if we came in and spoke to you and your wife for a moment?"

"The police? Why? What's this all about? We've always kept on the right side of the law over the years. Can't recall us doing anything we shouldn't have done. I'm perplexed as to why you should be standing on our doorstep."

Katy smiled. "It would be better if we told you inside, sir."

He stepped behind the door and gestured for them to enter the hallway. Stripped oak floorboards and magnolia walls greeted them.

He brushed past them and led the way up the long narrow hallway into a large kitchen at the rear. The kitchen formed part of an extension which included a large conservatory. Katy admired her surroundings, her envy gene on full alert.

This room is amazing!

"Darling, this is, sorry, my mind isn't what it used to be, DI Simpkins and DS Foster, was it?"

"The other way around but we'll answer to anything," Katy replied with a smile to put the couple at ease.

"Oh dear, have we done something wrong?" Mrs Simmonds asked. She wiped her hands on a tea towel and hung it over the handle of the oven.

"Why don't we take a seat?" Katy suggested.

The four of them moved to the dark coloured wood dining table in the conservatory. Mr Simmonds reached for his wife's hand and clutched it tightly. A lump appeared in Katy's throat. She was about to tell this nice couple that their world had been torn apart.

"Unfortunately, there's no easy way to tell you this, believe me, I've tried different ways over the years to break the unwanted news to relatives." Charlie nudged her knee under the table.

"Now you're scaring me," Mrs Simmonds said.

Her husband tore a tissue out of the box sitting in the middle of the table and handed it to his wife. "Please, whatever you have to tell us, get it over with."

Katy sucked in a large breath. "It is with regret that I have to tell you your son was found dead a few hours ago."

The couple faced each other and shook their heads. Tears slipped down Mrs Simmonds' flushed cheeks. "No, this can't be true. Not Bobby. Oh, God, not after losing Gina…"

Her husband shuffled his chair closer and rested his wife's head on his chest. "Hush now. Let's hear what the inspector has to say, darling."

"We've just been to break the news to his wife, she asked us to come and speak to you. I'm sorry this has come as such a shock."

"Oh, her. Bloody hell, I suppose she'll get the house now." Mr Simmonds spat the words out with venom.

Katy's interest piqued. "What are you saying, Mr Simmonds?"

"I'm saying they've been struggling for a few months to come to a conclusion on splitting up the house, don't you think it's a coincidence that all her problems are solved now that he's dead?"

"Robert! You can't go around making accusations of that magnitude. We don't know all the facts yet," Mrs Simmonds chastised.

Her husband sat back in his chair and folded his arms. "Go on, tell me she wasn't shifty when you spoke to her. Where was she when he died?"

"We questioned her about that. According to Anne, she was away from the house, staying with a friend."

"Ha! I rest my case. Pretty convenient, wasn't it? Don't answer that, I have my own theories about what happened and she would be right at the top of the list as a prime suspect."

"I'm interested to know why you should say that, Mr Simmonds. Has she ever threatened your son?"

"No, she hasn't. Robert Simmonds, you take that back this instant. Just because they fell out of love, it doesn't mean either of them would go after the other to get revenge. At least, I hope not. Anne has always been a quite reserved character in our eyes. She failed to integrate in the family, to embrace us as part of her extended family over the years. That's been a bugbear with us. I'm afraid what my husband has to say about her has been clouded by his judgement of the woman because of that fact."

"I see. We'll bear the information in mind, should any other evidence emerge in the meantime. I take it you were close to your son, is that correct?"

"Yes, very close to him. We were his parents." Mr Simmonds huffed out a breath.

"Robert, that was uncalled for, apologise to the nice police officer."

"I'm sorry. My mouth has a tendency to run away from me at times."

Katy nodded and smiled. "Accepted. What I was getting around to asking is, are you aware of your son having a dispute with anyone over the past few months?"

"A dispute? About what?" Mr Simmonds demanded. He turned to face his wife and they both shrugged.

"Anything, perhaps, with a neighbour or a falling out with a work colleague?"

Mr and Mrs Simmonds shook their heads. "No. What are you saying?" Mr Simmonds said, sitting forward in his chair.

"We believe your son lost his life in an accident, however, the pathologist has suggested that foul play could be involved just because of the injuries he sustained."

Mrs Simmonds gasped. "What… injuries? You haven't told us how he died, why haven't you told us that?"

Katy inhaled and let the breath seep between her lips. "It's a difficult one. We're a little in the dark as to how it happened. Our first assumption was that Bobby was knocked off his bike, however," she paused to choose her words carefully, "there were also tyre marks left on his face and body."

Mr Simmonds shot out of his chair and rushed to the sink. He turned on the tap, filled a glass with water and downed it in one go. "What are you saying? Someone deliberately drove over our son? That's inconceivable. Are you sure?"

"The evidence was there for all to see, Mr Simmonds. I'm sorry the news couldn't be better."

"Better as in, our son isn't really dead?" He returned to his seat and slumped into it.

"I'm sorry. It's a difficult job, trying to explain to loved ones how their relative has died. I appreciate you'll want to remember him as he was."

"Difficult? And you think the last ten minutes of you going around the houses has been a walk in the park?"

His wife placed a hand over his. "You'll have to excuse my husband, he's hurting and lashing out."

"Don't make excuses for me, love. I'm behaving the same way most parents would who have just heard their son has been killed. That is what you're telling us, isn't it?"

"Possibly. However, until the post-mortem has been carried and we have the report to hand, we will not be in a position to determine the facts, Mr Simmonds."

He shook his head and growled. "I can't bear the thought of him being cut open. You should be there with her... questioning her, inter-rogating her. Anne's the culprit, I would lay ten grand on it if I had the funds."

"You're talking nonsense as usual, Robert. Stop this. All you're going to do is cause the officers more work if you insist on suggesting Anne is involved."

"So what? What if it's the truth, love? Are you prepared to let her get away with it? With killing our son in order to gain financially? That's what this all amounts to. You have to investigate her if there's any doubt in your mind, don't you, Inspector?"

"You're right. We do. We've already checked out her alibi, sir."

He stared at her and fell silent. "In that case, we have nothing else for you. Our son generally got on with most people. We're distraught to learn of his death. Maybe if you leave us a card, we'll discuss the matter when you go; something might come to mind. It's the pressure of having you here, my brain has turned to mush. What about you, love?"

Mrs Simmonds nodded. "I agree. I'm finding it extremely hard to keep focussed right now."

"Okay, we'll leave you for now if that's what you want." Katy slid a card across the table and Mr Simmonds put his hand over it.

Katy and Charlie stood and said their farewells. "I'm so sorry for your loss. You have my assurance that my team and I will do everything possible to find the person responsible."

"Ha, don't forget to dig deep where Anne is concerned."

"Robert!" his wife warned.

He left his chair and showed them through the bungalow again. He refused to shake their hands. "I'm not kidding when I say this, Inspector, either you take my son's death seriously or I will take matters higher. Some of my best friends are ex-police officers and they still have contacts on the force."

Katy's head tilted to the left. "Is that a threat, Mr Simmonds?"

"Call it a warning. I know how these sorts of cases pan out; my advice would be for you not to cast this particular case aside, if you know what's good for you."

"It was nice meeting you, sir. We'll be in touch soon, should anything arise." Katy smiled even though she was seething inside.

She felt the waft of the door behind her when he slammed it shut.

"Bloody hell, that was uncalled for," Charlie mumbled.

"Come on, let's get out of here."

Charlie walked a few steps behind Katy. They stepped back into the car and Katy sighed heavily.

"Are you okay?" Charlie asked, concern written into the creases on her face.

"Yeah, he took the wind out of my sails. What the hell was that all about?"

"Maybe conducting an in-depth search into the family will reveal what his problem is."

"Can you make that a priority when we get back?"

"I'd be honoured. His anger was totally off the scale for me. Silly man, he might have just opened up a can of worms."

Katy sniggered. "You do amuse me, even when things are against us, you always seem to come out fighting."

"I do? I hadn't noticed. His attitude sucked, there has to be a reason why he turned on us in an instant."

"Ever the intrepid sergeant, I'm sure you'll discover the reason soon enough."

5

$\mathcal{A}$rmed with a coffee, Katy left the team doing the research and headed for the office. Needing to hear AJ's voice, she snuck in a quick call to home before she settled down to attack the onerous chore of opening the brown envelopes which were, thankfully at a minimum today.

"Hey, you, how are you enjoying your Saturday morning?" She sat back in her chair and peered up at the sun's rays radiating through the clouds overhead.

"You've just caught us. I asked Georgie what she fancied doing today and she's chosen to go to the adventure park in town."

Katy's heart skipped a beat at the thought of her baby exerting herself when she'd only just recovered from meningitis and the significant strain that had put on her already weak heart.

"Katy, are you still there?" AJ asked after a moment's silence.

"I am. Do you think that's wise, in the circumstances?"

"We can't wrap her up in a blanket all her life, sweetheart. I'll be extra vigilant with her, I promise."

"That wasn't a slight on you and your care for her, AJ. I just turned hot and cold within a few minutes there at the thought of her doing too much."

"I appreciate that. It's what she wants to do, who am I to stop her?"

"I want to visit Santa in Lapland mid-summer just to see what he does on his time off, but it ain't going to happen, AJ."

He laughed. "You've made your point. Sorry, but I'm overruling you this time. I hope that doesn't cause a rift between us."

"No, it shouldn't do. I trust you. I'm at fault for mollycoddling her unnecessarily. You go and have a good time."

"We will, and you wouldn't be you if you didn't question how I bring our daughter up at least once a week."

Katy's mouth dropped open, and a pain developed in her chest as if her husband had just plunged a knife two inches into her heart. "What? I don't."

He laughed, perhaps realising he'd gone too far. "Sorry, I was only joking."

Many a true word spoken in jest?

"I should hope so. I trust you implicitly, AJ, deep down you know that, right?"

"I do. Take it in the spirit it was meant, okay? Look, I have to go, Georgie is tugging on my leg to hurry up. I need to get her togged up, there's a slight breeze out there today."

"Okay. Take care and have a good time."

"What? No added *be careful* at the end?"

"That as well. I love you. Thank you for taking care of our daughter so well, just in case I don't say it enough."

"You do. We love you too, don't we, Georgie?"

"Yes, Mummy, love you. Daddy, I want to go now," her daughter shouted excitedly.

"I have my orders. Will you be home the usual time this evening?"

"That's the plan. I'll tell you about my day when I get home."

"Sounds ominous. Do you need to chat? I can hang around for another five minutes if you do."

"No, you go. I was only checking in on my two favourite people in this world. Miss you, have fun."

"We will. See you later."

Katy ended the call and sipped at her coffee, her mind full of anxious scenarios that might crop up for AJ and Georgie at the adventure park. She shook her head to dislodge the images and refused to visit them again for the rest of the day.

She left her office and brought the team together. They went over the facts they had in place and Katy transferred everything to two whiteboards, ensuring they keep both crimes separate.

"Over here, we have the first victim, Jason Davis, whose car was torched. We're aware what a vicious act that was and we believe we're on the lookout for this young woman. What do we have on her yet? Anything?"

The team's response was silence.

Dismayed, she shook her head. "I'm not liking your response."

Charlie raised her hand to speak. "What else can we tell you? No matter how frustrating it is, the crunch is we have nothing."

"Okay, let's set that case aside for now and I want to bring you up to speed on the other case Charlie and I attended first thing. That of Bobby Simmonds. From the snippets of information we've managed to gather from his soon to be ex-wife and his parents, it would appear that the man was perhaps mown down by accident and left on the road to die. Except the pathologist is suggesting a very different scenario, that Bobby was driven over a few times."

"Ouch, why? To be sure he was dead?" Patrick asked.

"Maybe." Katy blew out a breath and circled his name. "Here's what else we learned today, his parents are laying the blame solely at his wife's door. Our problem is that we've already checked out her alibi. She was staying with a friend when the incident probably happened."

"A friend who is willing to vouch for her whereabouts? From past experience, we know how that has worked out, right?" Graham raised a fair point.

"I know. That's why we need to keep digging. Not only that, his parents in a roundabout way turned on us while we were there. If I didn't know any better, I'd say they were doing their utmost to deceive us. I want to know what's gone on in the family's past. Maybe that's the key here. The next step in this case is for me and Charlie to go and visit his place of work. We could have stayed out there and done that this morning, but I felt I had to bring you guys into the action first. Therefore, I'm going to request the usual from you for both victims. We'll be working both cases at the same time. However, if one case turns out to be more worthy of attention than the other, well, we'll give that one precedence, of course."

"I'm just going to ask the most obvious question I can think of here," Charlie began, drawing everyone's gaze. "What if it turns out the cases are linked?"

Katy shrugged. "Of course it's a possibility, however, let's keep them separate for now until something definitive points us in that direction, Charlie."

Charlie seemed peeved. "Mind if I check social media, see if anything shows up? Just to satisfy my own curiosity."

"Go for it, if it'll make you feel better." Katy clapped and added, "Okay, you've got your instructions. I know it's Saturday and we're all a little jaded from working our butts off all week, but give it your all and hopefully we can get out of here early today. Don't quote me on that though." She smiled and dipped back in her office to retrieve her jacket. When she emerged again, Charlie was already standing by the exit. "Eager beaver."

*T*hey arrived at the B&Q store on the outskirts of town in a large trading estate. Katy produced her ID to the girl sitting on the reception desk and asked to speak to the manager. The young woman made a call and told them to take a seat. Sara watched a number of customers go through the tills and tried to figure out what they planned to do with their purchases. She nudged Charlie with her elbow. "Sitting here, watching all this activity involving DIY is making me feel guilty, our place could do with a lick of paint here and there."

Charlie sniggered. "Don't look. My place is the same but I refuse to feel either ashamed or guilty. We put in a lot of hours, Katy, I think we have a good excuse for not having the time to decorate."

"Thanks, that's made me feel a whole lot better."

A young man with greased back hair, wearing a suit, approached them five minutes later. "You wanted to see me? I'm David Evans, how can I help?"

Katy glanced around and leaned in, "Would it be possible to speak to you in private, sir? Perhaps in your office?"

His brow furrowed. He turned on his heel and called over his shoulder, "Come with me."

He marched off ahead of them, forcing Katy and Charlie to jog a little to keep up with him. "Bloody speedy Gonzales needs to effing slow down a little." Katy mumbled the complaint.

Charlie sniggered. "Tell him."

"Umm… Mr Evans, where's the fire?"

"Sorry?"

"Why the rush?" Katy asked. Her breathing rate escalated more than she had expected.

"Oh dear, having a problem keeping up, are you?"

"You could say that."

He threw them a smile and slowed down a touch until he reached the manager's office fifty yards ahead of him. "Take a seat. Excuse the mess, I have the big bosses descending on me in a few days."

"Ah, that explains a lot. We'll try not to keep you too long."

"Thanks. What's this all about?"

"Bobby Simmonds."

He leaned back in his chair and stared at Katy. "Go on. He's not here today, I've tried contacting him on his phone and at the house, but received zilch from both."

"I have to inform you that Bobby lost his life last night."

Evans bolted upright. "What?" he shouted.

"It's true. We're trying to figure out what his final movements would have been."

"I'm not with you. Why would you need to do that?"

"Mr Simmonds lost his life in an incident."

"An incident or an accident? I'm not sure I heard you correctly."

"An *incident*. He was cycling home last night and we believe he was knocked off his bike and killed."

"So it was an accident then?" Evans corrected her, seemingly confused.

"No. I can't really go into details, not because I don't want to, but because we don't really know what actually occurred until the pathologist has managed to piece things together during her post-mortem."

"Damn. I don't know what else to say. He was a good man. Very thorough in his job, the utter professional."

"What role did he have here?"

"He was my warehouse manager. He was pivotal in ensuring this place ran like a well-oiled machine. I'm going to miss him. He had a wicked sense of humour as well." A soft reflective smile developed.

"Maybe you can give us an insight into what his role consisted of and the hours he used to work?"

"He was in charge of stock levels in the warehouse, organising the stock once it had been delivered, that sort of thing. He locked up on a rota basis, together with the evening supervisor and myself on the odd occasion. It was his turn to secure the place last night, as it happens."

Charlie whipped out her notebook and started scribbling. "What time do you close?" she asked.

"We're open to the public until eight p.m. He would have left between eight-ten and eight-fifteen, I suppose. There were no notes left to suggest he stayed longer than necessary. Sometimes, he'll be delayed because a problem has arisen during his shift; he was professional enough to stay behind to sort anything out before heading home."

"I take it you have CCTV on site."

"We do. We also have an alarm system. I can verify the time he left by either means. Do you want me to do that?"

"If you could. Pinpointing the actual time would be a great start to our investigation."

"Give me a few minutes." He bounced out of his chair and left the room.

"It'll be interesting to see what shows up," Katy mumbled.

"Very," Charlie agreed. "It's not like we've got that much to go on so far, is it?"

"Sadly not. I detest cases like this, those that make us use our heads more than necessary, it's so damn draining."

They both laughed.

Evans returned to the room and requested they join him. He led the way down the corridor and into a small office which held several monitors. "I've checked back on the cameras. I'll hit the play button and you can see for yourself what happens next."

Katy frowned. "Are you saying you've found something of interest?"

"I'll let you be the judge of that." He ran the disc, it showed a few members of staff leaving at around five-past-eight and then Bobby Simmonds appeared, dressed all in Lycra. He locked the back door and set the alarm, then jumped on his bike. The cameras followed him to the front of the building. "Here's what I found."

Katy shuffled closer to the grainy screen. A car left its parking space and followed Simmonds. "Wait, can you tinker with the image? Home in on either the driver or the registration number?"

He tried his best, but the image, instead of becoming clearer, got progressively worse. "Sorry, no can do. You think he was being followed or could that have been just a coincidence?"

"I'm not sure. Do you recognise the car? Perhaps it belongs to a member of your staff?"

"No, sorry, I can't help you. All the staff are told to park in a designated area at the rear of the car park. This person, in my opinion, seemed to be waiting for him. Or is that my suspicious mind working overtime?"

"No, I believe you could be right. Would you mind creating a copy for us? We'll get it analysed and see if we can improve the image."

"Of course, I'll do it now. It shouldn't take me long, if I can remember how to do it. I think I'll need to refer to the manual." He searched in a nearby drawer, extracted a small booklet and flicked through it from back to front and the other way again. "Damn, I can't find it."

"Less haste more speed," Katy replied with a stiff smile. "Why don't I have a look for you?" He handed the manual to her, and she noted how much his hand was shaking. "Try and calm down."

"This is possibly the last time I've seen a colleague of mine and you're standing there telling me to calm down!" he snapped. His head dipped in shame. "Sorry, I shouldn't have said that. My emotions are twisted and all over the place."

"Don't worry, I'm the forgiving type in extenuating circumstances." Katy searched the reference index at the front of the booklet. "Here we go." She issued the instructions for Evans to follow, and between them, they managed to obtain a copy of the incident footage.

Evans ejected the disc and placed it in a plastic case, then handed it to her. "Glad to be of assistance. I hope this incident is an innocent mistake, can't stand the thought of knowing that the driver was intentionally following him. Umm… is it all right if I ask how he died?"

"All we can tell you at this stage is that he died in what we perceive to be an accident, involving his bike." Katy deliberately chose to keep the truth from him, conscious of his emotional state.

"How sad, after all he's been through this year as well."

"Sorry? Would you care to elucidate?"

"Going through the divorce from Anne, I meant. Another month or so and he would have been a free man and now he's gone."

"Are you telling me his marriage was a tumultuous one? I mean, we're aware they were getting divorced, but…"

"Oh yes, he used to come to work with the odd bruise now and again. When I talked to him about the issue, he always told me he'd bumped into things. I could tell he was lying. One day, I took him to one side and forced it out of him. He sat in my office and broke down in tears, admitted that Anne had been abusing him for years. I don't mind telling you that I was dumbfounded by his confession. I'm probably in the minority when I say this, I just didn't think women abused their husbands. Nagged them to death, yes, but physical abuse?"

Hmm… that would explain Anne's awkwardness during our conversation. "You'd be surprised. Was he getting any help?"

"From his doctor?"

"Yes."

"I didn't ask. The conversation was an awkward one. I broached the subject, but that's as far as it went. I dried up then, we both did."

"So you didn't discuss it any further?" Katy queried.

"No. I couldn't, I was out of my depth. I don't do relationships, you see. I'm a single professional who intends to climb the promotion ladder at the earliest opportunity. I can't do that if I'm tied down to a significant other, someone who could possibly get in the way of my success."

"I see." Katy waved the disc. "Well, thanks for this. We'll get it examined by our experts."

"I'll show you out. I hope the disc helps with your investigation."

"I'm sure it will. Thank you."

Charlie waited until they'd left the building before asking, "Will you take it to Forensics for them to try and enhance the image?"

"Yep, we'll shoot over there now. Maybe we'll strike lucky and find a tech available to do it on the spot."

They reached the car. Charlie paused and raised an eyebrow. "Is that wishful thinking on your part?"

Katy sniggered. "Maybe. We'll give it a try, let's face it, we've got nothing to lose. If we luck out, then we'll hand it over to one of the boys when we get back, see what they can come up with."

The lab was a fifteen-minute drive away from their location. Katy put her foot down when the traffic was at a lull, but most of the time, she found herself at a standstill, tempted to use the siren to get through the mind-numbing weekend roadblock. "Damn, and I thought it was bad enough during the rush hours around London, this is a nightmare to contend with."

"Yeah, I avoid coming into the city on the weekends, correction, I take the tube where I can, if I have to come in."

"Now you tell me. Thanks for that super useful nugget of information, partner." She was on the verge of doing a three-point turn when Charlie gestured for her to take a side street up ahead.

"I'm sure that's a short cut, might be worth a shot."

"We might as well. This is doing my head in. Why in God's name do people insist on bringing their damn cars in? I thought the congestion charge would have put paid to that line of thinking."

Charlie grunted. "Maybe people have got more money than sense around this area."

Katy inched forward until she could finally access the street. She looked in her rear-view mirror and snorted. "Follow my leader going on behind us."

"A mass exodus. I hope I'm right if not, there are going to be a few drivers pulling their hair out."

"That's the risk they take for following a woman driver, eh?"

"You have a nasty streak running through you, DI Foster."

Katy turned, grinned and winked at her partner. "Don't you forget it." Facing the road again, she asked, "Which way now?"

"Left then a sharp right."

Katy did as instructed and smiled when she saw the lab emerge in front of them. "Not just a pretty face, are you, Sergeant?"

"I've had my moments over the years."

Katy sniggered.

She found a parking space close to the entrance and they entered the building. The security guard grilled them for several minutes, and eventually, allowed them through.

Several technicians were chatting in the hallway. One of them looked their way. "Hello, ladies, can I help?"

"Possibly. I'm DI Foster and this is my partner, DS Simpkins. I was wondering if we could speak to someone about getting some CCTV footage enhanced. It's important that it's done ASAP as we have a possible murderer to try and trace, and well, this is the only clue we have to work with so far."

"Then you've come to the right place. Come with me. See you later, chaps." He turned and walked down the hallway with Katy and Charlie right behind him.

The corridor was endless, with a door on either side at regular intervals. Eventually, they came to a room near the end of it.

"Here we are. Let's see if Hudson can help you out." He poked his head into the room. "Can you spare five minutes to help out two damsels in distress?"

"What's it worth?" a man with a gruff voice replied.

"You'll have to ask them that, they're standing right behind me."

"Shit! Okay, send them in, I'll see what they need."

The man stepped to one side, smiled and motioned for Katy and Charlie to enter. He leaned in and whispered, "He adores helping people really, I promise."

"We'll take your word for that," Katy chuckled. "Hello there, I'm DI Foster, I wondered if you could do me a favour and try to enhance a grainy image we have, please."

The thirty-something man with blond spiky hair held out his hand. "Let me see what I can do. You want to wait?"

"We were hoping to, yes."

"Grab a stool. Grainy you said? What am I about to see?"

"Images of a man leaving work; he was later found dead. What we need to establish is who the person in the car that appears to follow him out of the car park is."

"Should be simple enough."

Katy and Charlie sat on the two spare stools and the three of them watched the image flicker onto the screen.

"Shit, this is really poor quality. If I manage to get anything clearer for you, it'll be a bloody miracle. Not the clearest footage I've seen over the years."

Katy grimaced. "Can you do your best for us?"

"Oh, I will. But I was just pre-warning you, doubt it's going to be good enough for what you need, that's what I'm saying."

Katy's gaze remained on the screen, emphasising her need to get on with things quickly. Hudson took the hint. He jabbed at a few keys and within seconds, the graininess dispersed and the image became a lot clearer. "Wow, that's amazing and you thought it wouldn't be possible."

"Okay, I've cleaned up the pixilation, we've still yet to see if it produces anything useful." He ran the disc for a few more seconds until the car came into view.

"That's what we need."

He concentrated his efforts on trying to highlight the vehicle and, before long he had homed in on the number plate, only for Katy to curse under her breath. "I should have known it would be too good to be true."

"Ah, yes, the old lay-thick-mud-on-the-plate routine. It would appear you have a very crafty killer on your hands, ladies."

Katy could have done without Hudson pointing out the bloody obvious.

"What about the driver? Can you possibly get a clearer image of them?" She crossed her fingers until it became painful as if resorting to some kind of personal torture as punishment.

"I can but try. Let's see what happens when I do this?" He prodded another couple of keys and all three of them stared intensely at the screen.

The driver came into view, sort of. There were no streetlights on the driver's side of the vehicle, only on the passenger side, therefore the driver remained in the shadows.

"Damn! Can either of you make them out, tell whether it's a male or female?"

Charlie shrugged. "I think it's impossible to tell from this angle."

"I have to concur." Hudson's tone was one of disappointment. "Let me have a fiddle for a few more minutes."

Katy watched him punch in a code or two, but nothing on the screen really changed. "It's utterly pointless, isn't it? We've hit a brick wall and it has frigging smacked us in the face, hasn't it?"

Hudson hitched up a shoulder and his mouth turned down at the sides. "Sorry the news isn't better."

"You've done your best. Thanks, Hudson. Is it possible for you to print us off a few of the clearer images? You never know, they might prove handy later on."

"At least you have the make and colour of the car, that's got to count for something."

Katy stared at the dark coloured Mini on the screen. "I wouldn't go that far. Is the vehicle black, dark green, dark blue, brown or what?"

"Ugh… okay, maybe the information is going to be as much use as a bag of crisps in a pig sty, then."

Katy wrinkled her brow at the analogy. "That's a new one on me, I won't even try to interpret what it means."

"Yeah, I shouldn't bother, my colleagues always take the piss out of me about using them. All I seem to do is confuse people."

Katy jumped off her stool and patted him on the shoulder. "Never mind, at least you tried."

The printer churned into life. Katy was expecting the usual black and white on grade B paper; instead, he printed out coloured pictures on glossy photo paper, not that it made much difference, given the crappy images they were working with.

They got back on the road and headed towards the station. "We're no further forward, are we? Which is bloody depressing, considering the amount of time we were caught up in damn traffic in our eagerness to get to the lab," Katy complained.

"Hard to figure out what's going on at this early stage. Want to know what I think?"

Katy shot her a quick glance and then refocussed on the road ahead once more. "Go on, don't hold back, never do that, Charlie."

"It sounds foolish, even to my ears. I wasn't about to spill my guts in front of a total stranger, the thought of being mocked rankles with me."

"No one would have mocked you for having an opinion. Come on, spit it out."

Charlie sucked in a large breath. "Well, I'm just throwing this out there, but I believe the two crimes are connected."

"You're going to have to give me more than that, love."

"Did you see the frame of the driver?"

"I couldn't really make out much, what are you getting at?"

"To me…" Charlie sighed. "It looked like the driver was either a woman or a slight male. Hear me out, bearing in mind that we're already on the hunt for a woman who we believe carried out the first murder."

Katy drummed her fingers on the steering wheel. "While I appreciate what you're saying, partner, I prefer dealing with the facts, otherwise we could be guilty of going around in circles."

"That's what I thought, which is why I tentatively voiced my opinion. There's another thing, the type of car seen on the footage."

"The Mini?"

"Yes, at the prospect of sounding sexist, isn't that car one of those more likely to be owned by a female? Or am I just reading things into it that simply aren't there?"

"No, I don't think so. It might be something worth considering, if there's nothing else really coming to light. Okay, let's go with that. When we get back to the station, why don't you do a search for Mini owners within a twenty-mile radius and see what comes back?"

"You're on. It's not like we have anything else vying for our attention at present, is it?"

"Hey, don't sound so despondent. It's par for the course to get dips and lows during an investigation, you should be aware of that by now."

"Yeah, I am. Just trying to do my bit to keep the momentum going. The last thing we need is things to turn stale at this early stage."

Katy smiled. "You're a good officer, Charlie."

*T*he rest of the day was spent discussing both cases and their similarities. It was enough for Katy to cautiously admit they should consider that the same person was responsible for both crimes. She cringed when she admitted that openly with the team.

"Is something wrong?" Charlie picked up on her disposition.

Katy tapped the whiteboard with the thick black marker a few times. "It's just that if our assumption is correct, then we could be on the lookout for a female killer. That in itself, doesn't sit well with me. Over the years, I've dealt with a few similar investigations, and I have to say, mostly, they turn out to be far more intelligent than their male counterparts. As much as I hate to heap praise on any type of criminals, if you get my drift?"

Graham shuffled in his chair. "I'm casting my mind back to Lorne's days with us, and yes, I'm inclined to agree with you, boss."

"Thanks for backing me up, Graham. Just because we think this person might have committed the two crimes, I still believe we should err on the side of caution, in case we're wrong. How's the research going, Charlie?"

Her partner rolled her eyes. "I'm kind of regretting my decision to take on the task. I've got a list of around a thousand to trawl through."

"Bugger. Can you narrow it down? Maybe just search for female owners on the list?"

Charlie laughed. "I have."

"In that case, double ouch. I've just had a thought." Katy paused and ran a plausible scenario through her mind. "Anne Simmonds... Patrick, do me a favour and find out what type of car she drives, will you?" Katy glanced at Charlie who was shaking her head. "Something wrong?"

"I'm thinking back to when we met her at the house, the only vehicle I saw sitting on the drive was a Ford Ka, not a Mini."

"Okay, that's dashed my proposal. There's still a possibility she might have borrowed someone's car."

"Maybe. I'll check what her friend, Jenna Brown drives," Charlie replied.

"Karen, what about the financial side of things? I appreciate it's the weekend, but any luck there?"

"Not as such. I thought I'd try and find out if Jason Davis had a life insurance policy on the go, but I'm struggling, might have to leave that until Monday."

"Fair enough. Okay, let's go down a different route, perhaps run both victims' names through the computer and see what that highlights."

"On it now." Karen turned in her seat and pounded on the keyboard.

Katy surveyed her team, all hard at it, and a sense of pride swelled in her chest. She was lucky to have such a diligent group of people surrounding her. There wasn't a single person she wouldn't trust with her life out in the field.

The searches continued until five when Katy decided it was time to call it a day. The team seemed both relieved and frustrated at the same time. Graham even volunteered to work late, but Katy turned down his request. "No, let's all go home and get some rest and come back on Monday, refreshed, Graham. I'll instruct the switchboard to contact me right away if anything suspicious arises. It's been a long week for us already."

Reluctantly, he agreed and said nothing further.

The team shut down their computers and left. Katy followed them out and locked the incident room, then she had a word with the desk sergeant on reception, told him not to hesitate to contact her should anything come to light over what was left of the weekend. She had her fingers crossed when she said it and hoped she wasn't tempting fate by uttering the words.

6

$\mathcal{M}$egan was sitting in her flat, flicking through the family photo albums of yesteryear. The year when her parents were still alive and their whole lives had been filled with an abundance of laughter and love. In the photos, Daniel had been a fully functioning child, running around the wild meadows, pretending to be an aeroplane and swooping low over their parents' heads while their mother prepared the picnic. What a feast that had been. She salivated at the thought of all the scrumptious pastries, the mini quiches, sausage rolls and pork pies. Everything homemade apart from the pork pies. When her father asked her mother why she didn't attempt to make them, her mother had laughed and announced life was too short to spend hours creating something that would be devoured within seconds. Marks and Spencer had done them proud there. For afters, they had mini swiss rolls and a plethora of different flavoured jam tarts. The simple plea-sures in life that, upon reflection, she missed so much.

It's their fault. All this heartbreak you've endured over the years. Look at what's happened to your brother, you think that's right? Get out there and avenge our deaths. Do it!

Her mother's voice made her jump. How did her mother always manage to pop up when she least expected it? Her nerves in tatters, she rocked back and forth for a few minutes and then snapped, "You don't realise the stress I'm under. Stop pushing me, Mum. You know how much I love you guys. I've already killed two of the bastards, please, don't start hounding me. I'm doing my best."

It's not good enough. We've waited an eternity to see those no-marks suffer. Why should they be allowed to continue to live their lives in full when they've stripped us of ours? Why? None of this makes sense. They served a pitiful sentence behind bars, why? Her mother's voice was fuelled by anger, becoming more high-pitched with every damning word, making Megan shudder.

Her mother wasn't finished, not yet. *Because of their bloody ages, that's what the judge said when he handed out their sentences. Two people they killed that day, the same day they robbed a family of a mother and father. I miss you and your brother so much.*

Tears sprang to her eyes, and she swiped at them, furious they had clouded the photo of her beautiful mother. "I miss you too, Mum, Dad. We'll be together again soon. I have a plan…"

Her mother's voice fell silent as if she was no longer around, except Megan knew differently; her parents were always around, gnawing away at her, chuntering on in her head. She had no peace. They emerged during her dreams, the nights she could sleep that was. She was tired, restless and exhausted, but, like she said, she had a plan that would deal with her tiredness once and for all when it came to fruition.

Megan nipped to the toilet. Gathered a few items she'd laid out on her bed and then pulled on her jacket. She left the house holding a carrier bag laden with equipment and drove to the destination. After parking in the car park of the wooded area, she took out her notebook and read through the notes she'd made a few weeks before when this whole scheme had begun to formulate.

With any luck, he should arrive soon.

She glanced around. The car park was empty just like it had been the other times she had recced the area, and a smile developed.

He came here three times a week, without fail. Jogged around the woodland, aware that it was safe to do so, except it wasn't, not today.

He was due within thirty minutes. *You'd better get a move on and sort your shit out, girl!*

Megan grabbed her carrier bag and headed into the dense forest. She located the designated area she'd chosen a few days earlier when she'd managed to run through her plan. He had been on his usual running schedule. She'd followed him there and set off after him to see which route he took through the forest. She'd been searching for an appropriate place to launch her attack and found it within a few hundred yards of the entrance. Now, all she had to do was secure her position before he arrived. He'd be here in twenty minutes.

With the dusk descending, she hid behind the huge oak tree and dived into her bag of goodies. She extracted the reel of nylon fishing wire and wound the raw end around the tree trunk, then crossed the path. Keeping the line low, just above the leaves, she placed the reel on the ground beside her. Then she unloaded the rest of the equipment from her bag in readiness and sat there, staring at the implements. Her mind running through what she intended to do with them once he arrived and fell into her trap. Adrenaline whooshed through her veins, adding to her excitement, or was that a bout of nerves?

She sat still for the next twenty minutes until finally she heard foot-falls coming her way. She picked up the fishing line reel and held it in both hands. A twig snapped in the near distance. *He's almost here, am I ready for this?*

Of course you are! Do it, we're here, we're right behind you. Give it to him. Make him pay for what he did to us. Rendering your brother a—

Just then her prey came into view. She closed her eyes for a split second, then chastised herself for being such a fool. She needed to concentrate, to devote every ounce of courage she had left within her to dealing with this man.

Another few yards and he'd be within range. He seemed as fresh as a daisy which caused her to pause. Maybe this was a mistake. Maybe she should have delayed her attack and set the trap towards the end of the circuit, instead of at the beginning. It was too late to change her mind now. She peered around the tree and saw him, her heart rate immediately trebling. Her chest inflated and deflated rapidly. *It's now or never.* She yanked on the wire and heard the man grunt and fall to the ground.

Megan revealed herself and pounced, not giving him the chance to get to his feet. In her plans, she'd assumed he would be less powerful lying on the ground. It was time to put that theory to the test. Armed with a cricket bat that belonged to her brother when he was able to run around and play, she ran at the man and started whacking him with the bat.

He cried out. "Stop it! What the fuck are you doing?"

She screamed and yelled profanities at him which increased her anger. A few bones snapped once the bat connected with its target properly. The man continued to yell at her, his tone a pathetic mix of fear and desperation. Then a foreign language emerged which caused her to pause for a moment.

"You fucker. You come to our shores and kill people. You're all the same, you come from war-torn places where losing a loved one is to be expected. It means nothing, does it?" She didn't have a clue what she was spouting, it just sounded feasible to her. The rage inside her bubbled to the surface, it guided her thoughts and her aggression. There was no holding back, not now that she had begun.

She bashed both of his legs, one after the other, with several hard blows. He howled in pain and tried to use his arms to defend himself, but she clattered his hands with the bat. A few of his fingers were now hanging at awkward angles. He placed his hands on the ground behind him and tried his hardest to crawl away, to escape her. But she was all over him, bashing him continuously with the bat.

Defeated, he pleaded with her to stop and then said one word, "Why?"

She paused mid-air and glared at him. "You don't remember me, do you?"

He frowned and, after a few moments of thinking time, he shook his head. "No. I'm sorry. I think you have the wrong person. Tell me what I am supposed to have done," he said, his accent thicker than before. Maybe that was the pain reflecting in his words.

"Don't take me for a fool." She battered his arm with several fierce blows.

"I don't know what you're talking about. Please, tell me."

"Eighteen years ago, does it ring any bells?"

His eyes widened and he instantly bowed his head in shame. "I regret that incident. It wasn't my fault. Anyway, I was punished for my part. How does it affect you anyway?"

"You killed my mother and father."

He gasped. "You're the little girl who survived."

"Yes, I'm the little girl who survived and has lived a life of torture. Reliving the crash time and time again in my nightmares, but that doesn't matter. This isn't about me. You killed them and left him... incapacitated," she screeched.

"Who? I don't know who you're talking about."

His continuous denials made her blood scorch her veins. She sneered at him. "There were two children travelling in that car that night, not just me. Daniel was in a coma for months. When he woke up, he was no longer the boy I used to chase around the garden for stealing my notebook and crayons. He was rendered brain damaged. You have no idea the suffering he has endured since then. His life expectancy has been cut in half. All because of you and your friends."

Fear widened his eyes. "No! It wasn't me. I had no control over what happened that night."

"Bollocks! You got in the car, didn't you? Out for an illegal ride in a stolen vehicle, never considering what the consequences might be driving a strange car."

"That's true. We were idiots. I'm sorry for your loss, for how your brother is now. If you let me go, I'll try to make amends. I have my own business, I can contribute financially to your brother's care. Please, let me do it. I'm not a bad person, I swear I'm not. All that happened in my youth, had it occurred today, I would have offered you and your family support. Take it, I'm offering it now. I can make sure he has the best nursing staff available to him."

Megan was seething inside, her lip curled and she spat at him, hitting him full in the face. "As if I'd ever take *blood money* from you. Daniel has the best care possible. We do everything for him, see to his needs, what's left of my family and I would never desert him. He's a part of us, no matter what state his body and mind are in now. We love him, he's still Daniel to us, that will never change."

"Good, I'm glad he has you to fend for him. Please, I want to help financially, to ease your burden a little. Won't you let me?"

"To ease your guilt, you mean. We've done all right without you up until now, what makes you think supplying us with money will do any good in the future?"

"It can help. Take it, take all I have. I can start over. I'm successful, I have the knowhow to create another business. Please, listen to me. If you love your brother, you'll accept what I've just put on the table for you, without question."

"How dare you! If I love my brother... what a thing to say after what I've already done for him."

"What's that? You care for him, yes?"

She leaned in, looked him in the eye and sneered, "I've killed for him and I'll gladly do it again, until I have avenged our parents' death, and how you and your friends left him."

The man shrank back, horrified by the impact of her words. "Isn't there anything I can say or do to make you reconsider?"

She shook her head, the anger building to a crescendo now. With the bat extended, hovering over his shins, she extracted a knife from the back of her trousers and raised it high above her head.

He held up his hand. Tears poured onto his cheeks. His lips trembled and his head shook. He pitifully pleaded for his life. "No, don't do this. Let me make it up to you. I have the money to give you everything you want in this life."

She'd heard enough. Megan screamed and plunged the knife into his chest, over and over again. She had no concept of time as she stepped back from the bloody mess. Surprisingly, there was no great sense of pleasure. She picked up her belongings, leaving the wire in situ, and ran out of the forest.

A couple rounded the corner and wished her a good evening. They got closer and stared at her and then glanced at each other with unspoken questions in their eyes.

Why would anyone come out here when the light was fading? Shit! Do I have blood on my face? She hadn't anticipated that. She hurried to her car and peered anxiously over her shoulder. They were heading in the direction of the corpse. She needed to get out of there, fast.

Throwing the carrier bag in the boot, she hopped back in the car and started up the engine. Suddenly, in her rear-view mirror, she saw the man and woman emerge from the trees. He was waving his arms frantically. Megan reversed the car, the red mist descended, and she drove at the couple. The man managed to jump out of her path, but the woman stood still, frozen to the spot. Megan yanked on the steering wheel, doing her best to swerve around the woman. There was a thud. She continued to drive, but glanced in her mirror once again to see the man run to the woman's aid. He lifted the woman's limp body onto his lap and rocked back and forth.

Megan burst into tears. What could she have done differently? Nothing, the couple shouldn't have been there. Now, instead of one corpse, the police would be called out to attend two murder scenes, each completely different.

You bloody idiot! Why run her over?

"Stop it! It wasn't intentional. I tried my hardest not to hit her."

You failed, didn't you? That woman was an innocent bystander. Your carelessness will lead the police to your door now. You've fucked up! Well and truly fucked up this time.

"I haven't, I'll get the final one sorted. Up my game. I'll go without sleep tonight if I have to. I have it all worked out. I have a plan that I'm sticking to rigidly, you'll see. I'll make you proud of me once more, I swear I will."

Ha, we doubt it. You've screwed up this time. The police will be on the hunt for you. Did you have to spit on him? Didn't you consider the impact of leaving the DNA evidence behind? Now, not only that, you've left a witness at the scene as well.

"I know. I'm such an idiot. What should I do?"

I would turn the car around, go back and finish the fucker off, but then, you're not me, are you?

Her mother's taunting added to her confusion. "No, I'm not. I won't do it. I refuse to kill another innocent person. She was a mistake that will live with me for the rest of my life."

Yadda, yadda. Innocent or not, they shouldn't have stuck their noses in. Turn around, go on, finish off the job properly. Or the police will hunt you down in no time at all.

Megan slammed her foot on the brake so hard she hurtled forward and bashed her forehead into the steering wheel. "Ouch! I will not have you calling me a coward, after all I've done already. How can you throw that one at me? How dare you?"

If the cap fits, daughter dearest!

Megan shifted into reverse gear and drove back to the scene to find the man still cradling his wife. He glanced up at her, fresh tears evident in his eyes. "Why? Why kill her?"

Megan was lost for words. She raised the blood-smeared cricket bat high and struck him in the head several times until she saw the light die in his eyes in the glow of the nearby streetlamp.

She trudged back to her car. With an exceedingly heavy heart, she left the crime scene.

7

*K*aty was in her car, heading home for the evening when her phone rang. She hit the button and the woman on control said, "So sorry to disturb you, ma'am."

"It's okay. What's up?"

"We've received a call from someone saying they found a body in the woods."

"Okay, isn't there anyone else who could attend?"

"That's a negative, believe me, I've tried, but they're all busy on other cases."

"And I'm not? I'm on my sodding way home, for fuck's sake." She grumbled and then offered an apology. "Sorry, you didn't deserve that. So, a body was found in the woods you say, where?" She searched ahead of her, indicated into a road on the left and pulled into the kerb to continue the conversation.

"Hawthorn Forest, do you know it? If not, I can send you the post-code for your satnav."

"That won't be necessary. I know where it is. Who found the body? It's usually a dog walker, am I right?"

"Not really. A man called it in, we dispatched an ambulance and a patrol car, but when the ambulance got there first, they contacted base to say there are actually three bodies at the scene, not just one."

Katy frowned. "How peculiar. Any sign of the man who made the call?"

"I thought it was odd as well. I tried to ring the number back and one of the paramedics answered the phone. The man was lying dead, holding his wife."

"How strange. Okay, I'll shoot over there now and try to fathom things out when I get there. Can you arrange for my partner, DS Simpkins to join me?"

"I'll give her a call now, ma'am."

Katy completed a three-point turn and drove back the way she'd come until she reached the main junction five minutes away. There, she took a right and continued for fifteen minutes until she arrived at the forest car park.

She let out a relieved breath. Patti was there and so was Charlie by the look of it. Katy pushed open her door and raced to the boot where she put on a white paper suit. She collected a set of shoe coverings and carried them to the edge of the scene. One look from Patti, warning her not to come closer, had her putting the covers on swiftly.

"What have we got?" she called out as she got within a few feet of Patti and Charlie.

"Do you want the facts or my interpretation of what happened?" Patti replied.

"Wow, that's unusual for you to have the lowdown on things so soon, we usually have to wait until you've carried out the PM before you divulge your theory."

Patti grunted, turned her back, walked past the couple lying on the ground and entered the depths of the forest which had been lit by her crew. They stopped alongside the bloody corpse of a man, surrounded by leaves.

"This is what I believe occurred. This unfortunate specimen of a man was hacked down, intentionally."

Katy stared at the man and shook her head. "How do you know that, Patti?"

Patti sighed and pointed at the thin nylon wire lying on the leaves which Katy had omitted to see. "A tripwire, in all senses of the word."

"Ah right, remind me to visit Specsavers the next time I'm in town, Charlie. That way I'll be sure to spot something that's staring me in the face next time."

Charlie chuckled, but knew to keep her mouth shut.

Patti glared at Katy. "Sarcasm isn't going to help this young man, is it, Inspector?"

"You're quite right, it isn't," Katy replied, slapping herself on the wrist. "Behave, DI Foster."

Patti ignored her and continued with her analysis. "The man was brutally attacked after his assailant tripped him up. He has several broken bones." She pointed to the shin bone breaking through the fabric on his left leg. "He suffered a sustained attack, perhaps involving dozens of blows from a hard object, which at this time remains unknown."

"So the culprit took the weapon with them? All we have to do is trace that person and hope they still have the weapon in their possession."

"Mock all you like, DI Foster, it's not uncommon for criminals to either dispose of the weapon or leave it at a crime scene, hence my reason for mentioning it."

"I was joking, Patti, I didn't mean to cause offence."

Patti ignored her and knelt beside the victim. She raised a gloved finger and traced a patch of wet on his face. "He was gobbed on, sorry, spat on, therefore, I predict we'll have genuine DNA evidence on this one."

"Makes a bloody change," Katy mumbled.

"I've taken a sample and sent it back to the lab already, because I'm efficient like that."

"I've never doubted your professionalism or efficiency before, Patti, so stop sniping at me."

"Just in case the thought crossed your mind. Anyway, as I said, the man suffered a sustained attack. Maybe he shouted out for help which angered his assailant more, hence the over-the-top thrashing he received. Going back to the other scene, mind your step, keep to the edge of the trees instead of the middle of the track to ensure we don't disturb other possible evidence, if you don't mind."

Katy and Charlie did as instructed and within a few moments they were back with the couple. "What's their story then, oh, Wise One?"

"This is pure conjecture on my part at this stage, but I've considered the scene carefully and feel sure I've made an accurate assessment, given the facts before me."

"Enough of the waffling, get on with it," Katy urged with the palms of her hands raised upwards.

Patti raised a finger in the air. "Here's my take on the proceedings, then. I believe the killer may have been interrupted by the couple, either as they entered the forest or as they were standing right here."

Katy frowned. "Why would the killer risk being seen in a public place like this? Do we know how popular this place is? What about in the evenings? Would you bloody go walking in the forest at night? I know I wouldn't."

"All valid questions."

"I have a suggestion, if you want to hear it," Charlie piped up.

Katy and Patti folded their arms and listened. "Go on," Katy urged, aware of how insightful her partner could be at intriguing crime scenes. Katy put this down to Charlie's time working with the K9 team and having to assess the scene thoroughly before setting the dog loose to track down a criminal or to search for an injured victim.

"What if the murderer, shall we call them, because, let's face it, that's what he or she is, after all, what if they were leaving the scene behind us and bumped into this couple? Fearing they might be able to identify the murderer, they decided to finish them off instead of just driving away from the scene."

Katy mulled her partner's suggestion over for a while under Patti's watchful gaze. "The cogs are turning." Katy grinned.

"I can actually see them gaining momentum," Patti added with a grin. "I have something else to say, if you'll allow me?" she added.

Brow knitted, Katy nodded. "Go on. What have we missed?"

"First of all, you need to listen to the original nine-nine-nine call. The man was the one who raised the alarm."

"Okay, what are you suggesting happened then?"

"The killer emerged from the woods, possibly bumped into the couple who were just going in for an evening stroll. Yep, I can't imagine why someone would come out here during the evening either, they had torches though." Patti pointed at a couple of pen torches on top of the exposed tree roots close to the couple's feet. "Anyway, my suggestion is that the couple discovered the other victim's body and maybe ran back to confront the killer. Foolish of them, given what's happened."

"Okay, and then the killer attacked them, perhaps while he was placing the nine-nine-nine call," Katy added, following Patti's line of thinking.

"Sort of. Look at the way he's holding her."

"It hadn't gone unnoticed, Patti, what are you getting at?"

She raised another finger and narrowed her eyes as she put her suggestion across. "What if, he rang nine-nine-nine and the killer decided to run, or drive off, I should say?"

"There's something you're holding back, what is it?"

Patti smiled. "You know me so well. I go back to what I initially said about the way he's holding his wife."

Intrigued, Katy said, "Go on."

"What if the killer, in their haste to leave the scene, mowed the woman down?"

"Hmm... is that likely? Maybe, I'm not sure. Okay, I'll go along with your scenario. What next? The killer returned to finish off the husband?"

"Maybe, that's the part that I'm finding perplexing at present."

Charlie jumped in. "It makes sense to me. Maybe the killer had every intention of driving off, getting away from the scene quickly, perhaps the woman jumped in front of the car to prevent the killer from leaving the scene. The husband was distraught, cuddled his wife, rang the emergency services to get the ball rolling. What if he was on the phone when the killer decided to return to get rid of any loose ends?"

Katy and Patti glanced at each other with raised eyebrows. Katy nodded several times. "Sounds mighty plausible to me. Charlie, get on the blower, ask to hear the nine-nine-nine call; we'll see if our combined theories match the events."

Charlie stepped away to place the call.

"Either way, it's a disgusting thing to happen," Katy admitted.

"I agree. I believe these two were innocent victims and that the killer has an agenda and was conscious about leaving any witnesses in their wake."

An excited Charlie rejoined them and put the emergency call on speaker. They heard a man asking for the police.

"Hello, police. It's urgent. We've just discovered a dead body and believe the killer is trying to get away. Please hurry, we're out at Hawthorn Forest."

"Please remain calm, sir. Is there somewhere you can hide? Perhaps secure yourselves in your car."

"No. We're on foot."

A revving car could be heard in the background. The man called out for Jackie to get out of the way. They heard a loud thud. The car roared away.

"Jackie, Jackie, are you all right? Please, hurry, the woman has just driven at my wife. I can't get a response. I think she's... oh God, she's coming back. Please, you have to help me!"

That was the end of the conversation. Katy swallowed down the lump in her throat. "My God, did I just hear him right? Did he say the killer was female and that she was getting away?"

Patti and Charlie both nodded.

"Fuckity fuck, you know where my mind is leading, yes?"

Patti and Charlie continued to nod.

Katy turned to face a tree and kicked out at its trunk. "Fuck!"

"You think the cases are connected, don't you?" Charlie muttered.

Katy swivelled on the spot to look at her and nodded. "Patti, what about you? There's been an underlying seed of doubt with us for a while about this."

"The similarities, the killer choosing remote locations and possibly intentionally stalking their prey, plus the fact that the killer is a woman, well, it's hard to deny. Maybe we should lump them all together and be done with it. Are you any further forward with the other cases yet?"

"We have a possible vague suspect to the second murder, but that's as far as we've got to date. We're hoping you can throw us a lifeline in the next day or two," Katy replied. She glanced down at the couple again. "Whoever the damn killer is, in my opinion, she's overstepped the mark killing this couple. Do you think she returned to the scene, possibly feeling a touch of remorse about the woman's death and then the husband having a go at her fuelled her anger and she lashed out and killed him?"

Patti shrugged. "Who knows? Only one person knows what truly happened. Sickening to think the killer has an agenda and isn't afraid to veer off when the necessity arises."

Katy shuddered. "The worst type of killer. We need to bloody track her down, quickly."

Charlie gave a brief nod. "I think we're all agreed on that. What next?"

Katy rolled her eyes. "The usual when we discover a body, the next of kin needs to be informed. Have you located any IDs, Patti?"

"One on the woman and her husband. Nothing as yet on the first victim. Maybe you'll get a little extra help in that department if someone reports him missing later."

"I'll tell the switchboard to let me know if they receive a call. Can I have the couple's IDs?"

"Help yourself, they're in the evidence bag over by the van."

Katy and Charlie left the scene and walked in silence through the wet leaves and snapping twigs to Patti's van. Katy bent to pick up the evidence bag and with her gloves in place she opened it and read out the address for Charlie to jot down.

"Are we going to try and find the next of kin now?"

"Yep, sorry. Did you have plans? I can tackle it myself if you want to go home."

"Not on your life. If you're out in the field, then so am I, we're partners."

Katy smiled. "We are that. I'm dying to see AJ and Georgie, but the guilt would tug at me if I didn't visit the relatives tonight."

"I'd feel the same. Want me to get in touch with the desk sergeant, see if he can come up with a relative for us to visit?"

"Good idea. I'll go back and see if Patti has anything else for us. I'll be back soon."

She walked the few feet back to the crime scene and spoke to Patti once more. "Charlie's conducting the search for a possible next of kin for the couple. I'm at a loss what to do about the single male victim, though. Any suggestions?"

"Apart from putting it out in the media, no, you're just going to have to sit tight for now. You've got enough on your hands to keep you busy for the time being, anyway."

"I know. But the thought of that man lying in a mortuary as a John Doe is tugging at my heartstrings."

"You old softie, you. I'm sure his identity will come to light soon. Now shoo, I need to get the three of them cleared for transferring back to the mortuary. Then I'm going to leave them and give up my Sunday to perform the posts."

Katy smiled her appreciation. "You're such a dedicated pathologist, not everyone would be prepared to put their life on hold the way you do."

"Get away with you. It's not like I have a tasty fella sitting at home, waiting to be ravished, is it? Unlike some I could mention."

"I know. It's a killer at times. I hate being so dedicated to my work. I'm lucky AJ understands."

"It's true, you've got one in a million there. Make sure you hang on to him and don't neglect him too much, eh?"

"I won't, I promise. Speak soon. Get the results back to me ASAP, I don't have to tell you that, do I?"

"No, you're right, you don't."

"See you soon, not too soon though."

Katy joined Charlie at her car and slipped off her protective suit. "Any luck?"

"We've got an address for the parents of the male, Fiona and Donald Ody."

"Where? Is it far?"

"About half a mile away."

"Okay, let's get changed and shoot over there. We'd better take both cars."

They jumped into their respective cars. Charlie led the way.

Ten minutes later, they had located a property on the edge of a large estate. They joined up again and approached the well-lit house. "Can't say I'm looking forward to what lies ahead. Have I told you lately how much I hate my job?" Katy grumbled.

"Only certain parts, I hope. You like it on the whole, right?"

"Debatable at times." Katy grinned. She straightened her face and rang the bell. "Here we go!"

A bespectacled man in his late sixties opened the door. "Hello, can I help?"

Katy and Charlie produced their IDs. "Hello, sir. I'm DI Katy Foster and this is my partner, DS Charlie Simpkins. I wondered if it would be possible for us to step inside and talk to you and your wife for a moment."

"May I ask why?" Mr Ody frowned and glanced over his shoulder as his wife appeared.

"Who is it, love?" his wife asked, her voice faltering slightly.

"It's the police. They haven't told me why they're here yet, so be patient."

Mrs Ody yanked her husband's arm. "Let them in. It must be cold outside for them."

He stood back and gestured for them to enter the warm hallway. "Thank you, it's a little chilly this evening. Still, it'll soon be spring."

"I can't wait, I love getting out in the garden in the evenings to have a tinker with the beds."

Katy warmed to the woman's friendly disposition, and her heart lurched when she thought about the task that lay ahead of her.

"Bungalows have larger gardens overall, don't they?" Katy asked.

The woman led them through to a cosy lounge, which was filled with tasteful oak furniture and autumnal colours decorating the windows in the form of blinds and curtains. Scatter cushions in matching fabrics completed the warming theme.

Mrs Ody sat on one of the single chairs, her husband sat in the other, and Katy and Charlie took a seat on the sofa opposite the couple.

"Now, perhaps you'll tell us why you're here on a Saturday evening?" Mr Ody asked, tilting his head to one side.

Katy gulped down the saliva filling her mouth. "We're here regarding your son, Christopher and his wife."

The couple shot each other a concerned look. Mr Ody faced Katy again, his brow furrowed and asked, "What about them? Are they in some sort of trouble?"

Katy rested her forearms on her thighs and clenched her hands together until her knuckles turned white. "This is so hard for me to say. Unfortunately, my partner and I were called out to attend a crime scene tonight." She paused to swallow again. "We received a call from your son earlier this evening to say he had found a body in the woods."

"Okay, so what aren't you telling us?" Mr Ody demanded.

Katy inhaled a steady breath. "We arrived at the scene to find your son and daughter-in-law both dead."

"What?" Mr Ody leapt out of his chair as his wife screamed. He sat on the arm of her chair to comfort her.

"I'm sorry, there's never an easy way to tell a relative about a loved one's passing."

"But how? How did they die?" Mr Ody raked a hand through his grey hair and shook his head in disbelief, all the while still comforting his wife who was swaying back and forth, sobbing her heart out.

"We believe, although it's pure speculation at this stage, that they discovered a murdered victim in the woods and possibly confronted the killer, who, rather than leave the scene, she decided that she would kill any possible witnesses."

"She! A woman did this?" he asked.

"Why? My beautiful son, why him? Why Jackie? They were such a wonderful couple, they did everything together. Put their family first, every day of their lives, and now… we'll never hear their laughter or feel their hugs ever again," Mrs Ody said between sniffles.

Her husband handed her a tissue. "Oh, Jesus, I can't get my head around this," he whispered. "What about Jackie's parents, have they been told yet?"

"Not yet. We came here first. Do you know them well?"

"Of course we do. They're an important part of our extended family. They live on the estate. Bought a bungalow a few doors down because we get on so well together. I'm going to give them a call, they should be here, listening to what you have to say."

Katy wasn't too sure that was a good idea at first, but after a few seconds' deliberation, she nodded, "I agree. Would you mind ringing them, Mr Ody?"

He squeezed his wife's shoulder. "Will you be all right, love, for a moment? They have a right to know."

"Yes, go. Don't ring them, go and get them."

"Would that be okay?" Mr Ody asked.

"I think it would probably work out better. Do you want my partner to go with you?"

He stood and walked over to the door. "I don't need babysitting. I won't be long."

"Donald, don't take your foul mood out on the inspector." Mrs Ody wagged her finger at her husband.

"I'm not. I'm allowed to be upset. I apologise if I came across abrupt, I've just heard my son has been killed. I'm not sure what the correct protocol is in such circumstances."

"You don't have to apologise to me, sir." Katy smiled to reassure him.

He left the room. Mrs Ody continued to cry.

"Can I get you a cup of tea, Mrs Ody?" Katy asked.

"Yes, if you wouldn't mind. Where would we Brits be without a cup of tea to cure us, eh?"

Charlie placed a hand on Katy's arm. "I'll get it."

"Thanks, Charlie. You're a good 'un."

Charlie closed the door behind her. Katy smiled at the woman, who was wiping her nose and eyes on a tissue.

"Does the pain ever get any easier? My heart feels like it's being torn out of my chest."

"It'll take a while to get used to not having them around. I'm so sorry to have to break such dreadful news to you, it's never easy finding the right words."

"I'm sure. Oh God, Vanessa is going to be distraught. Jackie was their only child, they adored her. Not saying we didn't adore Chris… oh, ignore me, I'm not making any sense." She stared across the room to the cabinet on top of which was a wedding photo of Chris and Jackie, and the tears started up again.

Charlie came back into the room carrying a tray with a mug of tea, a jug of milk and a sugar bowl. "I should have asked if you wanted milk and sugar."

"Thank you, just milk, please."

Charlie poured the milk into the mug and handed it to Mrs Ody, then she retook her seat next to Katy. "I didn't make us one."

Katy smiled. "It's fine."

They heard voices in the hallway and the door burst open. A woman and a man entered the room behind Mr Ody.

"This is… sorry, I've forgotten your names," Mr Ody, said, halting his introductions.

Katy stood and extended a hand to the couple who appeared to be perplexed by the situation. "I'm DI Katy Foster and this is my partner, DS Charlie Simpkins. Thank you for joining us. Please, take a seat." She motioned for Charlie to join her so the couple could take their places on the sofa.

"We're Vanessa and Zac Collins. Why are you here?" Zac asked as he and his wife lowered themselves onto the sofa.

It was understandable that Mr Ody had chosen not to fill the couple in on the short trip to the house. "It's with a very heavy heart I have to tell you that both Jackie and Christopher lost their lives today. I'm so sorry."

Vanessa and Zac stared at each other and then faced Fiona and Donald. "Is this true?" Zac asked, his voice straining a touch.

Mr and Mrs Ody both nodded. "Yes, it's true. Let me get you both a drink," Fiona said.

"I don't want a drink. I want my bloody daughter back," Vanessa shouted.

Her husband pulled her towards him, nestled her head on his chest and stroked her hair to soothe her. "There, there, love. We'll get through this. We're tough enough to cope with anything, remember?"

"Not this. When I said that earlier, I wasn't expecting to hear this. Oh, God, my poor child… gone, without us ever saying goodbye a final time."

"Isn't it terrible? They were murdered," Mr Ody filled the silence that had descended.

"What? How? No, I don't want you to go into great detail. I want to remember them as they were," Zac replied.

Katy smiled. "I would never go into detail. All I can tell you is that Chris made a nine-nine-nine call to say they had found a body in the forest. It's pure speculation on my part, but I believe the killer returned once she saw there were witnesses at the scene. Chris was holding Jackie in his arms when they died. The pathologist thinks that possibly Jackie was injured and Chris comforted her and then they both lost their lives."

"Why do you think the killer is a woman?" Mr Ody probed.

"Chris told the nine-nine-nine operator. Also, we have a few ongoing cases at the moment, which we believe we can tie together that are also pointing at a female killer. We've yet to get clarification on this, but the original victim in the forest fits the MO of what we're looking at with the other cases."

"Why haven't you found the woman yet?" Zac demanded.

"We've only been investigating the crimes for a few days. It takes time to gather all the evidence needed to locate a possible killer. Now we have three more victims to deal with which will probably hamper our efforts even more." Katy winced at the harshness of her words as they left her mouth. "Sorry, I never meant it to come out like that. All

I'm trying to say is that when another victim is found, the investigation process has to begin all over again. Such as tonight, coming here to tell you that your loved ones have died."

"Sorry to have caused you any inconvenience, Inspector," Zac replied stiffly.

"I can understand you being uptight, Zac, but I'm sure the inspector didn't really mean it to come across as heartless as it sounded," Mr Ody said in Katy's defence.

Katy gasped. "I didn't, I truly didn't. I can't apologise enough if that's the way it came across. Can I start over?"

"Please do, you've made a pig's ear of things so far," Zac grumbled.

Katy could have kicked herself, her inexperience of handling this particular task showing its awkward head again. "I can only apologise. It's not the easiest of duties, I can assure you."

"Give the girl a break, Zac. She's doing her best in a bad situation," Vanessa said, slapping her husband gently on the arm. "Please, can you tell us what happens next? When can we see them?"

"Yes, yes, we must see them," Fiona chimed in.

"Well, it'll be down to the pathologist to get in touch. She'll have to perform the obligatory post-mortems first."

"Why?" Fiona asked. "Why do they have to be cut up? I can't bear the thought of them being carved open."

"It's because of the nature of the crime, Mrs Ody. I'm sorry."

She shook her head and clutched her husband's hand. "Why them? Why did they have to go for a walk in the damn forest at dusk? Why not during the day like normal couples? Oh, don't mind me, my mind is racing. I have so many bloody questions running through it right now."

Katy offered the woman a weak smile. "That's understandable. Did they go to the forest regularly?"

"Yes, at least twice during the week and once at the weekend. There's a five-mile circular walk they take down there. You know, to keep fit. Well, look where that bloody got them in the end." She bowed her head and the tears slipped down her cheeks once more.

"No one could have foreseen this happening, Fiona," Vanessa said, softly.

"I know. It's me being silly as usual. I'm going to miss them both so much, especially with Melinda's wedding in a few weeks. Now, we'll have a funeral to sort out as well as the wedding. How on earth am I going to cope with that?"

Mr Ody squeezed his wife's shoulders. "We'll be here for you. There's no point thinking about that now, love." He glanced up at Katy. "Do you need to be here now? Shouldn't you get out there on the hunt for the killer?"

"If you're sure you no longer need us. I'll leave you my card, be sure to ring me if you need to discuss anything you might have forgotten to ask. Again, we're so sorry for your loss."

Mr Ody got to his feet and took the card from Katy, then walked into the hallway. "I'll show you out," he called over his shoulder.

Katy smiled at the other people in the room. "I'll be in touch as soon as I get any news regarding the killer."

"Make sure you do. Don't go burying your head in the sand on this one. I'll be keeping you on your toes by ringing you often," Zac warned, harshly. His wife slapped his arm again.

"Leave the poor young ladies alone. They have a tough enough job on their hands without you breathing down their necks."

He grumbled something indecipherable and sat back with his arms folded.

"It's okay. You have my assurance that we'll be putting in extra hours on this one," Katy promised them and then she and Charlie left the room to find Mr Ody standing at the front door, glancing up at the clear night sky.

"They'll be up there now, looking down on us."

"I'm sure. We'll be in touch soon, Mr Ody. Sorry to have met under such circumstances."

"Do your best to find the person concerned swiftly, for all our sakes, eh?"

"That's the plan, sir. Goodnight."

He closed the door gently behind them.

Katy and Charlie walked back to their cars. "What now?" Charlie rubbed her hands together to ward off the chill of the swirling wind.

Katy let out a long breath. "I can't go home, not knowing the killer is still out there. I'm going back to the station. No pressure for you to join me though, Charlie."

"I've told you before, if you're out here, then I'm with you all the way."

"I'm going to have to run things past AJ first. I'm also going to need to stop off and get something to eat. We haven't eaten for nearly seven hours, have we?"

"Around that time. I'll stop off at the chippie close to the station and catch-up with you, if you like?"

Katy opened her car door and dragged out her handbag. She flipped open her purse and took out twenty pounds. "No arguments, this one is on me. I'll have haddock and chips."

"Are you sure? I can buy my own."

"Do it. It'll make me feel better."

"Okay, on the proviso I buy the next one."

"Deal. Let's go. We have lots to do." She slipped into her seat and selected first gear.

Once she was back on the main road, heading back towards the station, she rang home. She'd rehearsed what she was about to say dozens of times, but when it came down to it, the words failed to appear. "Hi, darling. Bad news, I'm afraid."

"More bad news, you mean. What now, Katy?" AJ sounded pissed off, and rightly so.

"I was called out to a murder scene that turned out to be three murders, not just the one. I'm sorry, AJ. I need to tackle this one and stay on the trail of the killer. You understand, don't you?"

"I'm not some ogre, Katy, stop making me out to be one. Of course I understand your dilemma. I know how much you'd prefer being here, with us. It's your job. It's important to catch this person, but then again, you need your rest."

"I know. Charlie's with me. With both of us doing the legwork, we should have it wrapped up soon enough. I miss you and Georgie. I'm sorry for letting you down."

He snorted. "You've never let us down. Do what you need to do, we'll be here to welcome you home. Let's hope that's soon. Don't work yourself into the ground, love, nothing is worth that, you hear me?"

"I hear you. Thanks for understanding. Now I know why I love you so much. Not every man would be as accepting as you when it came to the crunch. I appreciate all you do for me, AJ."

"I know you do. You can make it up to me when you get home."

"You have my word on that, I promise. See you soon. Give Georgie a hug from me."

"She's in bed. Long past her bedtime."

"Sorry, no idea what the damn time was, not really."

He chuckled. "Go."

"I'm gone. Love you."

"I love you too, it's a good job, right?"

"It is."

8

With their bellies full of battered fish and chips, Katy bought them both a cup of coffee, and they got to work.

"Crikey, I'm that bloody full, you're going to have to give me a nudge now and then to make sure I don't drop off," Charlie complained. She flattened her hands across her distended stomach.

Katy laughed and placed the coffee on the desk in front of her. "We'll need to keep periodically nudging each other to ensure we're both awake, my damn eyelids are already drooping. Maybe we would have been better off sharing a portion instead of having one each."

"Definitely a case of our eyes being bigger than our bellies."

"Okay, let's crack on. Why don't we work until midnight and then call it a day?"

"Sounds good to me. Where shall we start?"

Katy stared at the whiteboard she'd brought up to date while she'd been waiting for Charlie to appear with their food. "Let's go through the background information together. I don't think the team have had time to really sink their teeth into anything as yet, not wishing to denigrate their efforts to date."

"It's been one of those weeks. The bodies have hit us hard and fast, and I don't think any of us could have imagined being inundated with so many perplexing cases in the space of a couple of days."

"Which is why I'm under the impression that the killer has an impeccable plan or agenda."

Charlie nodded thoughtfully. "I think you could be right. Okay, I'm going to look through Karen's notes." She stood and crossed the room to Karen's desk. "Oops, should I have asked for your permission before jumping in feet first?"

"No, it's fine. It makes sense and I'm sure Karen won't mind either. She's a team player, after all. Bring her paperwork over here and we'll both sift through it, if it'll make you feel any better."

Charlie grinned and nodded. "It will."

She gathered the A4 sheets Karen had stacked neatly on one side of her desk and returned to where Katy was sitting. She split the pile in half, handing six or seven sheets of neatly written notes to Katy while she retained the others. Katy had already flicked the switch on the monitor and the computer sprang into life.

Katy proceeded to carry out a basic search for the names of the victims in the archives, the ones they had, anyway. She read through the information on the screen and paused when something important caught her attention. "Jesus. What are the odds on that?"

Charlie leaned over and stared at the screen and then back at Katy. "Bloody hell!"

Katy pointed to the information halfway down the newspaper article. "He wasn't the only one involved in the crash, there were another three men in the vehicle when it sliced the other car in two."

"Mother and father killed instantly on impact and the two children survived. There are bound to be other articles in here about the accident, there has to be. Charlie, why don't you do a search on the database, see if any convictions come up?"

Charlie booted up the computer on the adjacent desk and shuffled her chair to settle behind it. It wasn't long before she let out a low whistle. "Bloody hell, I think I've hit the jackpot. I've got pitiful convictions for four young men: Jason Davis, Nikodem Nowak, Brian Timms and Ethan Romero."

Katy placed a finger against her cheek and muttered, "Hmm... okay, so no Bobby Simmonds? That's strange."

"What if he changed his name?" Charlie suggested thoughtfully.

"Hmm... you could be right. Hang on." She fell silent and searched her mind for a few seconds and then snapped her fingers. "I'm mulling over the conversation we had with Simmonds' parents. I felt something was off at the time. The way Mr Simmonds dismissed us as if he couldn't stand the police being near them, or was that my overactive imagination at play?"

"No, you could be right. There's one thing that doesn't add up, there's probably more than that really, but for now, if Bobby had changed his name, the parents would've been forced to do the same, wouldn't they?"

Katy tapped her finger against her cheek. "Might be worth another visit if nothing else shows up. Something is definitely amiss here. First of all, I think we need to do all we can to find out what we know about the men. Christ, if it's here in the archives, then the information is open to the public, that could be how the killer has got hold of the information." Katy put her hand over the mouse and moved it. "Wait, scrolling through, I have a photo of each of the four men. However, I don't think they're going to be much use as the accident happened over eighteen years ago."

Charlie left her seat and stared at the screen. "Let's take Jason Davis first." The pair of them viewed the man from different angles and agreed. He looked much the same except for his shorter hair.

"Okay, here's Brian Timms, does he look familiar to you?"

Charlie tilted her head and enlarged the man's photo using the mouse. "I'd say there was more than a passing resemblance there, yes. Wait, let's set that aside for now, maybe there'll be a photo of him with his parents later on which will validate our assumption."

Katy smiled. "You're good. Okay, let's put him to one side. What about this man, does he look familiar to you?"

"As in the victim found in the forest earlier? No, I'm not feeling it, are you?"

"Nope, I was about to say the same. That leaves this man, Nikodem

Nowak." Katy enlarged his image and stared at it for several moments. "What do you think? A possibility?"

"I'd say so. He has distinctive eyes, even if the image is in black and white."

"You're right. Let's do some research, see what we can find out about him. No, to save time, I'll do that, why don't you see what shows up for the fourth man, Ethan Romero? I've got a good feeling about this Charlie." Katy was buoyed by what they'd discovered so far.

"Me too. Does that mean we get to go home earlier than anticipated?"

Katy chuckled. "You never know your luck."

They both set to work, pounding their respective keyboards. Katy's adrenaline flowed at a fair pace through her body, as if leading the charge to find the information that would be the key to breaking the case.

"Aha! What do we have here? According to this article written at the back end of last year, Nowak is an award-winning restaurant owner in the area."

"He is?" Charlie frowned and queried.

Katy glanced up at the clock, it was already ten-thirty. She reached for the phone, dialled the number of the restaurant and held her crossed fingers up in the air as she waited for her call to be answered.

"Hello, Toskas. Can I help you?" A young female voice with a slight foreign accent filtered down the line.

"Oh hi, yes, I hope so. Is Nikodem there, please? If so, I'd like to have a brief chat with him."

"Who are you?"

"Sorry, I should have introduced myself. I'm DI Katy Foster of the Met Police. Is he there?"

"No. I don't know where he is. It's a mystery, he usually shows up just after we open, at around seven, but tonight, he nowhere to be seen. I tried calling him, but his phone just rings and rings and then goes into voicemail. I've given up trying to contact him now. He must be out having nice time with a girl. Sorry, ignore me, I shouldn't have said that."

"I won't tell him what you said. So, am I to understand he's not married then?"

The girl let out a real belly laugh. "Him? No way. No woman would ever be able to tie him down, many have tried over the years, or so I've been told. He goes out with a woman for a maximum of six months before he dumps her. He prefers life alone rather than be tied down, is that how you say it?"

"It is. Perhaps you can give me an address where I can contact him?"

"Why? Me no like handing over personal information to someone over the phone. You could be trying to trick me."

"I'm not. I promise. My concern is genuine for Nikodem."

"I still not sure. You come here in person, let me see your ID before I hand over information. How about that?"

"I could do that, but it's only going to prove a waste of time. Please, just give me his address."

Silence filled the line for what seemed like eons. The girl tutted on the other end. "Wait a minute. I wouldn't do this usually, but I must admit I'm worried about not being able to get in touch with him. He's always available twenty-four hours a day. He loves this place and finds it difficult to let go."

"I understand. His address, if you will?" Katy prompted.

"Just a moment. I need to get my mobile, it's in my contacts." She dropped the phone on a desk, so Katy presumed, and returned less than a minute later. "Here it is. Forty-one Turnpike Close. Do you know it? It's not far from the restaurant. He insists it would be a better idea to be on hand, just round the corner, in case of emergencies."

"I'll look it up on the map. Thanks for your help."

"It's okay. I hope he doesn't have a go at me for giving out his address."

"I'll make sure you don't get into trouble, you have my word." Katy ended the call and looked at Charlie who had raised an expectant eyebrow. "Well, according to the young lady, he hasn't shown up for work this evening, which is a rarity. I have his address, but it's not going to be any use, he hasn't got a girlfriend or partner. Sounds like a

Polish Casanova to me, or he was. From what she told me, I'm making the deduction this is him, our third victim. I'll try and ring Patti." She reached for the phone.

"Umm… you think that's wise at this time of night? She'll hang, draw and quarter you if you wake her up. By the sounds of it, she doesn't really get a lot of sleep as it is."

"See, I told you, you're a wise officer. In that case, maybe I'll leave it until the morning. How have you got on? Any luck?"

"Ethan Romero is an IT consultant with Dorett Bytes. That's all I have on him really, except reading through that article he was the driver of the vehicle."

"Was he now? Let me take another read through the editorial before we decide what to do next."

Charlie left her to read and bought them both another cup of coffee. "You read my mind, thanks, hon. Jesus, considering these guys were joy riding and the devastation they caused, they sure did get off lightly. Maximum term served was by Ethan, he got four years. The others ended up doing three years each."

"Shameful. Why is it driving offences tend to carry a lesser sentence than a murder conviction when it amounts to the same thing? In the wrong hands, i.e., joy riders, a vehicle can be classed as a lethal weapon, can't it? Why don't judges see it that way?"

Katy blew out a large breath that puffed out her cheeks and she tucked a few strands of hair behind her ear. "Your guess is as good as mine. It's always been the same as far as I can remember."

"It's disgusting. Those poor kids weren't taken into consideration at all, not in my eyes."

Katy found herself nodding in agreement. "The courts were far more lenient eighteen years ago. Thinking about it, I'm not sure hit and runs or joy riding accidents are taken any more seriously nowadays." She paused and mulled over something which flicked through her mind. "There was that case recently where a mother and toddler were killed outright when that young driver swerved to avoid hitting a dog. He climbed the pavement instead and knocked them down. If I recall rightly, the driver pleaded his innocence in court only to be handed down a five-year sentence for manslaughter. Two lives snuffed out in an instant, and that warranted five years sitting behind bars?" She sighed and shook her head in dismay. "He could be out in two and a half years, what kind of message is that sending out to the general public?" Her heart raced as she thought about another high-profile case that had angered her. "And don't get me started on that US diplomat who fled the country after running over and killing that young man. I feel for his parents; on top of the grief they're experiencing, they're having to travel the globe to seek justice for their son. Diplomatic immunity sucks, big time. That woman shouldn't have been behind the wheel of that car in the first place. I hope she rots in hell."

"Maybe Biden will step up to the plate and force her to take the punishment, there's no way Trump would have had the guts to speak out against the woman. He was such a stubborn president, who regularly dug his heels in when people tried to either force him into a corner or pleaded with him to do the right thing."

"Yeah, I hear you. A total power freak. So glad the US people finally decided to vote him out. Anyway, enough of putting the world to rights, I'm thinking we should take a drive out to see this Ethan Romero."

Charlie raised an eyebrow. "At this time of night?"

"Why not? If he's the only survivor of the four, I think it's imperative that he should be warned of a likely imminent danger, don't you?" Katy switched off her computer and stood. She slipped on her jacket and headed for the door.

Turning off her own monitor, Charlie joined her. "You've got a point. Let's hope he's at home. Should we try calling him instead?"

"Nope. It's all or nothing right now, I don't think we should take the risk."

"I suppose you're right."

*E*than Romero seemed pissed off to see them standing on his doorstep. He refused to let them into the house, going as far as to bar the way with his muscular arms. A female appeared and peered over his shoulder. "Who are they?"

"It's the police, Donna. Let me handle this, go back inside."

Katy picked up on the fact that he was warning the woman to go inside rather than asking her politely to leave. "Is something wrong, Mr Romero?"

"No. Should there be?"

"Not really. Anyway, if you wouldn't mind answering a few questions, we'll leave you in peace to enjoy the rest of your Saturday night."

"What sort of questions? I know nothing about anything that should involve the police."

Katy smiled. "Is that right? Let me cast your mind back to the accident you were involved in all those years ago. Can you remember?"

His eyes narrowed and Katy noted him chewing on the inside of his mouth. *Is he nervous, or angry at being confronted about his past misgivings?*

"What about it? It was a long time ago. An incident I've done my very best to forget about over the years. I did my time as punishment for my sins."

"You did. You served what? Two years in total. Not much of a sentence considering the outcome of the accident, I'm sure you'll agree."

"The sentencing was out of my hands. We had a great barrister who believed in us. What more can I say?"

"Let's move on from that travesty and debacle of a sentence to the present day. Tell me, are you still in contact with your fellow joy riders?"

He glared at her for a moment or two and then shook his head. "No. We stopped speaking to each other in prison."

"You did? May I ask why?"

"Believe it or not, we were all riddled with guilt. It wasn't our intention to kill that couple and destroy their family unit."

"I see. If you were torn up with guilt, why did you bother hiring a top brief?"

"Wouldn't you in the same situation? You're not making any sense asking such a dumb question."

"Sorry if you believe it was a dumb question, I'm simply searching for the facts."

"Why? Why raise the incident again now, after almost nineteen years? And yes, I'm still counting the years off on my calendar."

"Glad to see the accident has impacted your life in some minor way."

"How dare you! What's the meaning of this visit? Either you tell me in the next five seconds or I'll shut the door on you."

"Touchy, aren't you, Mr Romero, may I ask why? Has someone been in touch with you to put you on edge?"

"What twaddle are you on about? I haven't got a clue what you're going on about."

"And you're sure you haven't seen your fellow joy riders in the last few days or weeks?"

"Stop calling them that, they have names, use them."

"All right, I will. Brian Timms, now going under the name of Bobby Simmonds, Jason Davis and, last of all, Nikodem Nowak. Have you been in touch with them lately? Please answer me truthfully, it's very important."

"Tell me why."

"I asked a question first. Please have the decency to answer me."

"It's late. Unless you're here to arrest me, I suggest you leave me alone."

"By the way you're avoiding my question, am I to take it you have been in touch with some or all of these men?"

"No. Now go!" He cast an anxious glance over Katy's shoulder and closed the door.

"Damn. I should have been prepared for that and shoved my foot in the gap."

They turned to walk back to the cars. Charlie sighed and suggested, "It's late. Why don't we call it a night? At least we know he's safe, for now. I didn't like the man, did you?"

"I didn't like his attitude, that's for sure. Maybe I should have tried harder to have warned him."

"Possibly. In your defence, he was being quite offhand with you."

"Hmm… we'll see what tomorrow brings. I'm only going to put in half a day, though. Do you want to join me? Will Brandon be okay with you giving up your entire weekend to be at work?"

"It won't be all the weekend, not if we finish at lunchtime, although that remains to be seen, knowing our luck lately."

Katy sniggered. "Yikes, how true that is. Okay, I'll see you at around nine in the morning. Thanks for going the extra mile to be by my side today, Charlie. It's truly appreciated."

"I know it is. I couldn't let you do all this alone now, could I?"

"You're the most conscientious partner I've ever had, apart from your mother, that is."

"Good genes and all that. See you in the morning."

Katy waved goodbye and watched Charlie drive away. Her gaze drifted to the window on the first floor where she spotted Ethan Romero staring out of the window at her. He turned and started shouting at the woman who had also come to the door. It was clear they were arguing as he was wagging a finger at the woman and Katy could hear their raised voices, but couldn't make out what they were saying.

Romero closed the curtains, but the shouting continued. Katy decided to leave the couple to it and jumped behind her steering wheel. On the way home, she recapped the conversation she'd had with the man who refused to allow them access to his home. *Why was that? Did he have something to hide? Could he be behind the other murders? Had one or all of the men pissed him off recently and he'd taken revenge by doing away with them? No, that can't be right, can it? We're looking for a woman. What about his wife, or the woman at the house? Could she be the woman who had killed the others and the two innocent walkers? Was that even feasible?*

During the drive home, despite feeling tired, the questions reverberated around in her mind without the answers revealing themselves.

She wearily parked the car and opened the front door of her home.

AJ entered the hallway and leaned against the doorframe to the lounge. "How are you doing? You look shattered. Have you eaten?"

After slipping off her heels and coat, she padded across the hallway and planted a kiss on his lips. "Yeah, I'm still stuffed. Charlie and I ate a whole portion of fish and chips each. I think I'll stay clear of the scales tomorrow."

"Nonsense, there's nothing to you. I made a cottage pie, but we can all share it for lunch tomorrow, it's no big deal."

"That'll be lovely. Umm… I have a confession to make."

His mouth twisted from side to side. "Go on, surprise me."

"I have to work in the morning." His shoulders slumped and his head dipped. She placed a finger under his chin and pulled his head up again. "I'll be home by one, I promise."

"Why don't I believe you, Katy?"

He stood upright and went into the lounge. Sensing there was about to be an argument. Katy followed him into the lounge and closed the door so they didn't wake Georgie. "AJ, you know I wouldn't entertain going in on the weekend if I didn't think it was necessary."

"You need to have some time off. I'm not a grouchy bugger, you know that, but bloody hell, love, what will it take for you to show us some consideration now and again?"

Stunned by the acidity in his tone, Katy's mouth hung open. She recovered and shook her head. "Love, let's not do this now. I had every intention of not coming home until midnight, but here I am…" She glanced at the clock on the wall and winced. It was eleven-forty-five. "Ouch, where did the time go?"

"See, you have no concept of time. Your daughter was in hospital last month and you've barely spent any time with her since she came out. I've had to put my own business on hold to care for her."

Ashamed, she nodded and whispered, "I'm sorry. I have so many balls in the air right now."

"You need to sort out what your priorities are, Katy. I'm not having a go at you, adding to your stress, all I'm asking is that you take a step back now and again and think about your family. You've become too reliant on me picking up the pieces."

She gazed into his eyes and saw only sadness there. Katy hesitated for a moment, willing him to open up his arms to draw her in. It never happened. In the end, she mumbled another heartfelt apology and retired to the bedroom.

AJ joined her ten minutes later. It worried her how he chose to cling to his side of the bed, not daring to let their bodies touch. Katy turned to face him. Taking the initiative, she slung an arm around his waist and shuffled closer. She kissed his bare back. Glad that he neither flinched nor tried to shrug her off; that was a good thing, wasn't it?

He let out a long sigh and she whispered yet another apology. AJ turned in her arms, his face an inch or so away from hers on his pillow. "If I didn't love you so much, all this would be so much harder."

Tears welled and she smiled. "I promise to do better. Manage my time better and not to let work dominate my life as much from this day forward."

"Stop!" He pulled her closer and snuggled into her neck. "Don't promise something that is out of your grasp to fulfil, Katy."

"I'll see to it. Make sure this type of thing doesn't happen again. We're so close to breaking this case though, you know how it is. But if it comes down to the job or losing you and Georgie, then I know the sacrifices I need to make, sweetheart."

"The last thing I want is to force you into choosing between us and your career, I'm not the type to bully, you know that. Forget I said anything, I'm concerned for Georgie's sake, that's all. She spent most of the day asking why Mummy doesn't want to spend time with us any more and it touched a nerve."

Katy gasped and could do little to prevent the tears spilling onto her cheek. "Ouch! Out of the mouth of babes. Honestly, once this case is over, I'll try not to let work get in the way of our time together again."

"Okay, just be aware that broken promises affect us all."

He kissed her, a long, deep kiss that did everything to reassure her that their relationship would stand the test of time… if she stood up to her end of the bargain and spent more time with her family.

9

*G*eorgie joined them in bed the following morning, something that was becoming a habit on a Sunday. It made Katy's heart sing to have her family around her, if only for twenty minutes or so. She kissed her daughter on the head and caressed her hair.

Katy jumped in the shower while AJ and Georgie went downstairs to prepare her a special breakfast to set her up for the day. She groaned inwardly, her stomach still full from eating the damned fat-laden fish and chips the day before.

She spent an extra five minutes with her family after breakfast was finished and then drove to the station. Charlie was already at her desk, the computer screen on, and making notes.

"Hey, stop! You're putting me to shame." Katy teased and Charlie laughed. "Sorry I'm later than intended. Georgie wouldn't stop nattering this morning and it made me feel guilty leaving her when I should be at home on a Sunday. The things we do to keep crime off the streets, eh?"

"Aww… poor Georgie. It must be hard for her to understand and even harder on you to leave her and AJ for the day."

"The same could be said about you and Brandon. Everything all right there?"

Charlie waved her hand from side to side. "It's as well as it can be, I suppose. Once this case is over, Brandon's insisting we should sit down and discuss our future."

Katy slotted a coin in the vending machine and prodded the white coffee button. "Sounds ominous." She placed the cup on Charlie's desk.

"Thanks. I'm used to it. He's always putting the pressure on, but when it comes to the crunch of actually discussing our problems, he tends to shut down."

Katy returned to the machine to fetch a coffee for herself and then sat down next to Charlie. "I'm sorry, love. I'm always here if things ever get too tough for you."

"I'm fine. Does it give a bad impression for me to say that I'm used to it?"

Katy shrugged. "It doesn't bode well for a relationship, does it?"

"Nope, Mum would say the same, if I ever confided in her. I'm trying my best not to go down that route. The last thing I want to do is cause her to regret moving to Norfolk."

"I hear you. After this case is over, why don't you and Brandon go away for a few days to try and put your relationship back on an even keel?"

"I think it's too late for that. Do you mind if we stop talking about it, Katy? It's nice to be at work, doing my best to forget all the angst I'm having to deal with at home right now."

"Sure, that works for me. Let me nip into the office, see what post is in there, if any, and then we'll get stuck in."

Charlie pointed at her desk. "I'll continue with what I was doing. My mind refused to shut down last night, so I thought I'd come in early to chase up something that's bugging me."

"Can't wait to hear what it is. Two secs and I'll be back." She dipped into the office and peered at her in-tray. There was a smaller pile than usual. Small enough to make her mind up for her. She backed out of the room and rejoined Charlie, whose fingers were darting across the keyboard. "Right, let's have it."

Before Charlie had a chance to speak, the phone rang. Katy answered it on a nearby desk. "DI Katy Foster, how may I help?"

"Please, please, you have to help us. He's gone, she's taken him."

Katy instantly put the phone on speaker. "Okay, one thing at a time. Who is this?"

"Donna Platt. We met yesterday, you came to our house."

Katy stared at Charlie and mouthed, "Do you know the name?"

Charlie shook her head and opened up a search screen on the computer.

"I'm sorry. I don't recall your name," Katy replied, perching on the edge of the desk behind her.

The woman growled. "Ethan Romero's fiancée. All right, we were never introduced, but you were at the house last night."

"Ah yes. Okay, you said something about someone being missing, who are you talking about? Ethan?"

"No, it's our son, Matthew. She took him. Told us if we contacted the police that she would kill him. I haven't slept all night, I can't stay silent a moment longer. Please, you have to help us."

"When did this person take your child?"

"Yesterday, around two in the afternoon. He was playing football at the park with his friends. I was late picking him up, I had a puncture. I'm pretty sure she did it to make me late for collecting him. It was her plan to kidnap him all along."

"I'm so sorry to hear this. Is that why Ethan was off with us last night?"

"Yes, we argued most of the night after you left. I pleaded with him to tell you, but he refused in case she carried out her threat."

"Where is Ethan now?"

"Out there, searching for them. I couldn't stand the stress any longer. We need your help, we'll never get Matthew back without your assistance, I'm sure of that. But... I'm terrified to think what will happen if she hears that I've been in touch with you. You can't put this out in the news, I'm begging you."

"Please, don't worry. Where was your son playing football? We'll see if there are any cameras on site or in the vicinity."

"There are, I've seen them. They've had problems with the centre being vandalised over the past few years. It's the Tom Fordyce Centre." She let out a deep sigh. "It was set up in the young lad's name. He lost his battle to cancer and the money raised from his charity contributed towards building the facility."

"Thanks. We'll get on to it straight away." Katy motioned for Charlie to action it. "This woman obviously contacted you, what were her exact words? Has she made any demands, you know, for money?"

"No. She told us she had him. This is all about revenge. Ethan is beside himself and I'm... well, I'm frantic, going out of my mind with worry. What if she hurts him?"

"Revenge? Did she say what type of revenge?"

"The revenge *type*. I don't know. Ethan doesn't know either, I've tackled him about it."

"Seems strange that she should come after your son, is it likely to be a case of mistaken identity?"

"No! Oh, I don't know. Ethan's no bloody help whatsoever. I'm going out of my damn mind. Please, can you help us?"

"We're going to do our best. Did the woman tell you her name?"

"No. But Ethan is acting weird, as though he's aware who the woman is, but is refusing to tell me."

"Well, we believe we have a rough idea what this is about."

"I wish someone would bloody enlighten me then, because I'm floundering around in the dark here."

"Are you aware of Ethan having a conviction?"

"He said he went to prison on a minor matter in his teens, but that's all he's ever told me. What did he do?"

"He and three other men were found guilty of manslaughter after the car they'd stolen ploughed into another car, killing two adults. Two children survived the crash."

"Oh, shit! I had no idea. So who is the woman?"

"We haven't quite figured that part out yet. My partner and I have come into work on our day off to do some extra digging into the case."

"There's an obvious connection though, that's what you're telling me between the lines, right?"

"We believe so, yes. I need you to prepare yourself for what I'm about to say next."

"Shit! Okay, I'm ready."

"This week we've been investigating the deaths of three, actually five, people." Donna gasped. "Three of those people were involved in the same accident Ethan caused. He was driving the vehicle at the time."

"Holy crap! And now this woman, whoever she is, has my son!" Donna sobbed, unable to contain herself any longer.

"So it would seem. I'm sorry, Donna. Please, try and hold it together, I realise how difficult that's going to be for you, but we're getting close, you have to take my word for that."

"Who is this fucking woman? Why take my child as punishment?"

"We're working on it, I promise you. The way things stand, I'm inclined to think the woman is possibly a relative of the family involved."

"But it was an accident!"

Katy sighed. "An accident caused by joy riders. That has to hurt."

"Oh, God. I don't know what to say or think any more. Please, I just want my baby back, you have to help me. He doesn't deserve to be held responsible for his father's sins. I hate Ethan for keeping this from me. I had a right to know, damn it, look where it has led now. I could have kept my son out of harm's way, had I known. Bloody hell, you think I would still be with Ethan had he been honest with me? There's no way on earth I'd still be here today. My son is innocent, you have to help me to get him back. He's my world. Please."

"We're going to do our very best. What I'm going to need is an up-to-date photo of Matthew."

"I can send it via my phone."

"Good. I'll give you my number." Katy told the woman her mobile number and waited for the picture to appear. "I've got it. We'll print it out and distribute it. Try not to worry."

"Please, if she finds out I've spoken to you…" Donna's voice trailed off and a sob filled the line.

"Please, try and remain positive. We'll take every precaution to keep your son's involvement quiet. One last thing, can you give me Ethan's mobile number?"

Donna gave the information and Charlie jotted it down.

"Okay, I'm going to crack on with things now. I want to thank you for bravely reaching out. I also want to assure you that we'll maintain discretion at all times and issue a warning for our colleagues to do the same."

"Thank you. Please, please bring my baby home safely."

"I'll be in touch soon." Katy ended the call and then sent Matthew's picture to the printer. "I won't be long, I need to get this down to the desk sergeant right away."

"I'll keep digging into what's going through my mind, I'll hopefully have something for you by the time you get back."

From the doorway, Katy shouted, "Do you think we should summon the rest of the team?"

"I don't think we have that much to go on, let's see how we go for an hour or so and reassess."

Katy nodded and raced down the stairs two at a time. She found the weekend desk sergeant standing at reception. "Hi, Stan, I have an urgent task for you."

"What's that, ma'am?"

She went through what she expected of him. He listened intently and actioned her instructions immediately. "Leave it with me."

"Remember, you need to emphasise to your men the need for discretion. If this woman gets wind that we're onto her... well, I dread to think what the consequences might be."

"Don't worry, I'll be sure to let them know."

"Keep me informed of anything and everything, okay?"

He nodded and Katy hurried back to the incident room. She sat next to Charlie. "Phew! Quite an eventful day already." She gulped down the remainder of her lukewarm coffee. "One of these days, I'll get to drink a hot cup around here. Go on, what is it you want to share with me?"

"I think Donna has burst my bubble on that front. You know we came away from Ethan's house wondering if he and Donna were behind the killings? I think we can put that scenario to bed now unless Donna is trying to pull a fast one, leading us astray."

"Hmm… not sure about the last part of your theory. She seemed far too upset to me, plus, there's the fact that the news about Ethan's involvement in the crime totally blew her socks off."

"That's true. Okay, we need to take a different approach in that case. Look at a possible family member carrying out the murders."

"Which is what I said to Donna, and I stand by that. Did you have someone in mind?"

Charlie scrolled through the article she had on the screen, about the crash, and circled a section right near the end. "I found this more up-to-date piece regarding the crash. The daughter, Megan, was four at the time, she escaped the crash with just cuts and bruises. However, her brother, who was seven at the time, was in a coma for several months. When he emerged from the coma, he was paralysed."

"Oh fuck! That's a shocker! What are you saying? You think it's Megan?"

"I don't want to believe it, but it would be interesting to track her down and have a chat."

Katy nodded, her head gaining momentum the more she mulled over the plausible development. "If she's close to her brother, maybe seeing him suffer all these years has finally taken its toll on her. Add to that the fact their parents died in the crash and…" She puffed out her cheeks. "I have no idea how that woman must be feeling. What if she's her brother's carer? It might have finally sent her over the edge. What do you reckon?"

"Possibly. Want me to dig a little more?"

"Yes. Try and find her address, it'll be worth paying her a visit. Maybe, if she is the guilty party, we'll find the missing child at her home."

"If she's the primary carer, wouldn't she be taking a risk?"

"Kidnapping is a risky strategy full stop, whether you're caring for someone with disabilities or not."

Charlie rolled her eyes. "Yep, I get that. Give me ten minutes."

Katy brought the nearby computer to life and stared at the article about the case, her eyes focussing on Ethan. She punched his number into her phone. It went to voicemail. She left an obscure message about him contacting her and waited for him to call back. That call hadn't materialised by the time Charlie asked for her full attention once more.

"I've located an address for Megan. Is it worth us popping around there?"

"Where is it?"

"A flat in Islington."

"What level, do we know?"

Charlie suggested it might be on the seventh floor, which made Katy a tad wary.

"Would she be able to care for a disabled person if she was seven flights up? What if the lift broke down? Don't they usually place vulnerable people on the ground floor?"

"Possibly. We won't know until we get there and see for ourselves."

Katy sprang out of her chair and glanced up at the clock. "It's already eleven o'clock, I promised AJ I'd be home by one without fail."

Charlie twisted her mouth. "It'll be pushing it."

"Sod it. I sense we're close, Charlie. We need to follow our instincts on this one. I'll dodge the bullet with AJ when I get home. Use my womanly powers to disarm him if need be."

Charlie sniggered. "You're such a courageous woman."

Katy slapped her on the top of the arm. "Stop taking the piss. Let's go full throttle on our quest."

They switched the computers off and tore down the stairs. Outside, the sun was poking its head through a thin cloud. It was good to feel its warmth on Katy's back, it had been a long winter they'd had to contend with. Spring and the summer ahead were something to look forward to. She'd make it up to AJ and Georgie in the coming months.

. . .

*T*hey arrived at a run-down block of flats that was at least ten storeys high. Katy stared up at the dark grey monstrosity and tutted. "They don't make them like they used to, thank God. What was the architect bloody thinking when he designed this atrocious excuse for community living?"

"I dread to think. Maybe it was a bet."

Katy laughed. "Come on. Let's go have a chat with Megan Johnson."

Charlie paused. Katy peered over her shoulder. "Cold feet?"

"Not really. Maybe we should have brought backup with us, or at least we should tell someone where we're going. As it stands, only you and I know we're here, we'd usually have the rest of the team armed with that knowledge."

"Good point. I'm guilty of racing ahead as usual. I'll let the desk sergeant know, get him to ring me if he doesn't hear from me within the next thirty minutes, how's that?"

"Sounds like a plan to me."

Katy continued walking towards the lift at the same time she placed the call. The sergeant agreed to spring into action if he hadn't heard from her at the allocated time.

"Ah Jesus, I should have known the frigging lift would be out of order; it always is in dives like this," Katy complained. They trudged up the concrete stairs. Each time they reached another level, she glanced out at the dismal view, grateful that she lived in a semi in a nice street with her family. This estate truly was the pits.

"It's a good job we're fit. Can you imagine trying to get someone confined to a wheelchair up and down these stairs?"

"I doubt if it would be possible. Maybe the brother prefers to be indoors all the time. Let's face it, this estate isn't really conducive to going out for a nice stroll around the neighbourhood, is it?"

Charlie cringed. "You said it."

Once they reached the seventh floor, they paused for a moment or two to catch their breath. "I think it's this way." Charlie pointed to the right as the landing split off in both directions.

"I'm happy to take your lead. Have you got your pepper spray handy?"

They'd already donned their stab vests after leaving the vehicle. "Yep, in my jacket pocket. Maybe we should have brought a Taser with us as added security."

"Too late for that now. And that's another thing we need to sort out, your Taser training."

"I'm up for that, although I'd rather have a K9 to hand."

Katy grinned. "I'm not usually keen on being so close to a German Shepherd, but I'd gladly have one standing alongside us right now."

Charlie smiled and they continued along the litter-filled balcony. Charlie pointed at a group of needles over in one corner.

"Disgusting, why am I not surprised, given our environment? The sooner we get out of here the better, this place is giving me the heebie-jeebies." They stopped outside the flat they were after, and Katy covered her hand with her sleeve to knock on the door.

Unfortunately, the door remained closed. She had to risk it, she rapped on the door with her bare knuckles, but that too proved to be a waste of time. "No luck. Either she's not home or she's choosing to ignore us."

"Worth asking the neighbours?" Charlie suggested.

"You go left, I'll go right." Katy took three steps and knocked on the door to the next flat.

The door was answered quickly by a young woman with bright red dyed hair. She wore a low top and shorts. "Yeah!"

Katy produced her ID. "You haven't done anything wrong," she added quickly, sensing the woman was about to shut the door in her face.

"Damn right I haven't and neither has he, for a change. What do you want? Be quick, the kids are wanting their breakfast."

"I'll be quick. I'm making enquiries about your neighbour, Megan Johnson."

"Who? Which side is that? We keep ourselves to ourselves, best way around here."

Katy pointed to next door. "Do you know much about her?"

"Not really. See her now and again. Never spoken to her."

"Can you tell me if she lives alone?"

"Nope. Next question."

Katy resisted the temptation to heave out an impatient sigh. "Have you seen her with anyone else?"

By this time the woman was looking totally bored. "Nope. Next."

"What about someone who is disabled?"

"Are you taking the piss? How would someone get up here in a wheelchair when the lift never bloody works?"

"Okay, I'll leave you to it. Thanks for your…" The door slamming shut in her face prevented her from finishing her sentence.

She marched back to see if Charlie had fared any better with the other neighbour. "Thanks, that's a big help. Sorry to have disturbed you."

The old lady, bent over slightly with age, smiled at Katy as she joined them. "That's all right, dear. I like to do my best where the police are concerned. I never know when I might need your services."

"Thanks all the same. Enjoy the rest of your Sunday."

"You too, although saying that, you're working, not much fun for you, is it?"

"We get by," Charlie replied.

They walked away and started down the stairs. "How did you get on?" Katy asked.

"The woman said she knew Megan well enough to say hello to, but couldn't really give me much in the way of useful information."

"That's a shame. I got the same reaction from the other neighbour, sort of. Did you manage to ask her if Megan's disabled brother lives there as well?"

"I asked, but the woman couldn't give me a definitive answer."

They reached the car before either of them spoke again. "Jump in, let's get out of here."

Charlie slid into the car and fastened her seatbelt. "Where to now?"

"Back to the station to put our heads together."

"About the brother?"

Katy turned to her and nodded. "Amongst other things."

They both remained lost in their thoughts during the twenty-minute journey back to the station. Katy had Charlie well-trained by now because as soon as they entered the incident room, her partner homed in on the vending machine to buy the coffees.

Charlie placed a cup in front of Katy who had already booted up the computer. "I'm out of my depth a touch on this one, you know, with regard to the brother being disabled, it's not something I've had to deal with either professionally or personally before. Do you have any knowledge on the subject?"

"No, not really. I'm sure we can work it out between us."

"Ha, it could be a case of the blind leading the blind then, hang tight." Katy blew on her drink and took a sip. "Let's see what Google can come up with when I type in 'where are disabled people likely to live?'"

Charlie leaned over to view the search results. "I suppose it depends on the severity of his condition."

"Yep, you're right. He could be in an assisted-living place with support on site or he might be living independently, if he's only partially disabled. Ugh… see, told you I'd be out of my depth, is there such a thing as being partially disabled?"

Charlie smiled. "I don't think so. A person is either disabled or able-bodied, in my opinion."

Katy rolled her eyes. "Of course. Glad I said that to you and not someone else who would likely take offence."

Charlie looked at the results on the screen again. "There's another option that isn't listed up there."

Frowning, Katy asked, "Go on, what are you thinking?"

"That possibly another member of the family is caring for the brother."

"They'd have to be an absolute angel to put their own life on hold for someone who wasn't their immediate family, I mean either the parents or a sibling. Maybe they had another brother or sister, perhaps? Can you recall the article mentioning that?"

"No, I don't think so. What about an aunt or uncle, perhaps? Do we know who took on being the kids' guardian after the parents died?"

Katy brought up the article and between them they scan read it to try to find the answer, but unfortunately, the information wasn't listed. "Damn. Where the fuck could we find out?"

"Would it come under Social Services? I'm not sure, I'm just throwing it into the mix."

"Possibly. I have a contact there." Katy dashed into her office and found her friend's number. She returned to the incident room, flopped into her seat and dialled Tania Quinn's mobile. It rang several times and then went into voicemail. "Bugger, nice to know someone gets a Sunday off, unlike some I could mention."

In the meantime, Charlie had carried out a search of her own and come up with an emergency number for Social Services. She picked up the phone and rang the number. "There has to be someone on call, whether they'll be able to divulge the information or not is another matter."

The automated system ran through different options, none of which were beneficial to them. Instead, Charlie remained on the line in a queue until she spoke to an actual person. She was caller number ten.

"Wonderful, so much for this being an emergency number, what if someone was desperately in need of their help?" Katy grumbled. She picked up a pen and tapped it on the desk.

"I suppose if someone is desperately ill, they would need to ring nine-nine-nine or one-one-one. Again, I might be talking out of my arse."

Katy chuckled. "You always manage to brighten a dull day."

She stared at the clock, it was coming up to twelve-fifteen and they'd been on hold, listening to what was supposed to be soothing music, for more than ten minutes. She left her seat to stretch her legs. "This is driving me bloody potty."

A woman's voice came on the line. "Social Services, how may I help?"

Charlie sat back in her chair and motioned for Katy to reply. "Ah, yes, sorry to trouble you. I'm DI Katy Foster, I'm in need of some information."

"You're aware this is an emergency hotline and not an information service, aren't you, Inspector?" the woman said abruptly.

"Yes, and I apologise, but this really is a matter of life and death. We have a kidnapped child we're trying to trace."

"I see. What do you need from me?"

"We're at a loss as to where to turn. We're trying to contact the family of the person we believe may have kidnapped the child. The woman in question has a disabled brother. As far as we're aware, he doesn't live with her. What we need to find out is where the brother lives. It's our only way of tracing this woman."

"I understand. I'll see what I can do to help. What's the brother's name?"

One hand held up with her fingers crossed, Katy replied, "It's Daniel Johnson. There was an accident eighteen years ago, their parents were killed outright. Daniel was in a coma for a while and then classed as disabled after the accident."

"Just a moment, I'll input the information to see what I can find."

"Wonderful."

"Ah yes, here we are. I thought I recognised the case. A terrible shame for the kids to contend with. According to our records, the aunt and uncle offered to care for Daniel and Megan. As far as I can tell, they're still caring for Daniel."

"Marvellous. I don't suppose you'd be willing to give me their address, would you? It's imperative we find out where Megan is."

"I'm going to need you to send me some form of ID first, I can't possibly hand over such sensitive information at the drop of a hat, I'm sure you understand."

"Totally. How do you want to do this?" Katy said, trying her hardest not to grit her teeth at having to jump through hoops for this woman.

"I need you to scan your warrant card and send it to the following email address. That way it'll come straight to me and I can action things immediately."

"Scan it? Won't a photo of my card via my phone do? The technology is more up to date than having to hunt around for a scanner. I'm not even sure the printer in the office scans documents et cetera."

"It does, I can do it for you," Charlie whispered.

"Okay, ignore that. My partner said she's willing to give it a go."

"That's perfect, problem solved. If you give me your number, I'll ring you back once I've received the email from you, and we'll go from there."

Katy jotted down the email address the woman gave her and let Charlie do her bit regarding the scan. "What a bastard, having to prove who I am over the damn internet."

"It's better to be safe and all that. Can you imagine the number of calls they have to contend with? Fake calls at that."

"All right, you've convinced me again. How long is it going to take?"

"Less time if you persist in asking me questions."

Charlie worked her magic with the computer mouse and the scanner and before long, a light traced a line under the lid.

"All the years I've been here, I just thought it was a damn printer."

They both laughed. Charlie sourced the document from the computer, attached it to an email and hit the send button.

Within seconds, the woman from Social Services was on the line, verifying that the documentation had been substantiated.

Thank fuck for that! Not sure what I would have done if she'd rejected it. "Great to hear. Now, about that information. You know, what with time being of the essence and all that jazz."

"There's no need to be grouchy, Inspector, we all have our protocols to adhere to, as you're well aware."

"I am. Can we get on with this, please?"

"Very well. The children were placed with their Aunt Gail and Uncle Sam. Their address is number eight Whittaker Close, East Finchley. Do you need the postcode?"

"If you wouldn't mind."

The woman read it out and Charlie entered it on a clean page in her notebook.

"That's very kind of you. I don't suppose there's anything on their records that we should be cautious of, is there?"

"Wait, I'll just check. No, I don't believe so. Apart from Daniel being severely disabled. He has problems communicating with the family."

"How sad. Okay, we'll take it easy when we go and question them. I can't thank you enough for your help."

"My pleasure. I hope you locate the kidnapped child. If you hadn't mentioned that, I doubt I would have been so willing to divulge the information, not over the phone and definitely not on a Sunday."

"So glad you took pity on me. Enjoy the rest of your day."

"Ha, I doubt it. Good luck."

Katy hung up and her gaze was immediately drawn to the clock. It was getting ever closer to one, with ten minutes to spare.

Reading Katy's mind, Charlie said, "Would you rather visit them tomorrow?"

"I would, however, my conscience refuses to allow me to even consider putting it off. I'll give AJ a call on the way. I doubt he's going to be happy with me, although under the circumstances, a child going missing, I'm hoping he'll at least be a bit more understanding than usual."

"Good luck with that one."

They switched off the computer and slipped on their jackets.

"What about Brandon?" Katy asked as they raced down the stairs and out to the car.

"Nah, I won't bother. I have more important things on my mind than being subjected to silent treatment. I'll suffer his wrath once I'm at home, face to face is always better than delivering the news over the phone. It is in our relationship, anyway."

"I know things will be a thousand times worse if I don't ring AJ. Here, you drive, that way I can concentrate on pacifying him without fear of causing an accident." She threw Charlie the car keys.

Charlie smiled, adjusted the driver's seat to suit her longer legs and drove out of the car park. Katy inhaled and exhaled a few times, doing her best to try to calm her racing heart.

"Hi, AJ, it's me."

"Are you on your way home? If so, I'll put the dinner on."

She closed her eyes, imagining his hopeful face and beaming smile on the other end. "No, believe me, I'm so sorry to let you down at this late stage. Something major has transpired and I have to visit someone urgently."

"It's fine. Don't worry about us. Georgie, go get your coat on, sweetheart, we're going to McDonalds for lunch."

Georgie screeched in the background and Katy's heart sank. She hated that place. She'd always been brought up to think of McDonalds as supporters of the IRA back in their heyday and had avoided spending her well-earned money there over the years. She tried her hardest not to react, but it was an impossible task.

"Can't you go elsewhere? You know how I feel about that place, AJ!"

"Exactly, which is why we avoid it when we're with you. Georgie and I love going there, we just never tell you when we have a sneaky burger and chips."

"What? Do you realise what you're saying? You're teaching our child to be deceitful, you think that's right, AJ?"

"Don't start on me, Katy. I care about my daughter and her needs."

"And you're saying I don't? How can taking her out to McDonalds like that be caring for our daughter?"

"What time should we expect you home now?" AJ swiftly changed the subject.

"I don't know. I'll give you a call later on."

"Don't bother, we probably won't be here. I'll take Georgie out for the day to make up for you not wanting to be with her."

"AJ! Where the hell is this coming from? If you only knew what we were up against here, you'd be encouraging me to remain at work and do my best."

"You have made it perfectly clear where your priorities lie over the past few weeks, Katy. Things are going to be changing around here. I've decided that Georgie needs at least one adult in her life who prioritises her well-being. I'm volunteering to be that person. Let's face it, she can no longer rely on you, can she?"

Tears pricked Katy's eyes and she shook her head. "You're not being fair, AJ. I wasn't going to tell you this for fear of it upsetting you, but what the heck… we have to remain out in the field on this one because as it stands, we have a child who has been kidnapped. I don't want to get into a long drawn-out debate about this, I'm putting another child's life before my own. I think on this occasion, it's warranted, don't you?"

"Umm… you should have said sooner."

"You reckon? You didn't give me a damn chance. Go, AJ, have your damn burger and manky fries from that place, I hope you suffer the consequences later."

"Bloody charming." He ended the call.

Katy jabbed at the button. Her leg bounced up and down as her anger grew. "I never expected that. What is wrong with him? I'm out here, on my day off, trying to keep this place safe, a safer environment in which to bring up our child and he slates me for it."

Charlie gave her a sympathetic look. "It's because he cares so much about you and Georgie. He wants to spend time with you and is bitter that you're devoting too much time to your work, it's only natural, Katy."

"If he hadn't been a copper once upon a time, I could completely understand where you're coming from, partner. But he knows what we have to endure in order to bring down some of these criminals. You name one criminal we've arrested since you've joined us who committed all their crimes between the hours of nine to five?"

"I understand your frustrations, I truly do. But on the other hand, you need to recognise AJ's point of view as well."

She sighed, feeling defeated. "I do. I swear I do, especially with Georgie's condition always rattling around in my head. Maybe I should take a leaf out of your mother's book and bloody retire!"

Charlie bashed her hand against her thigh. "You can't do that! I know Mum threw in the towel a number of times, but she also returned to her role a couple of times too, because she needed to feel wanted. To achieve the maximum results throughout her career, to maintain the balance in her life. That's how I perceived it, anyway. Don't be like Mum, you're going to need to take a step back, delegate more if necessary, if that's what it takes to keep your marriage alive."

Katy shrugged. "Maybe it was the wrong call for us to tie the knot. Anyway, what made you so damn wise, young lady?"

"I think you know the answer to that one, boss."

Her leg stilled and she inhaled her final deep, calming breath. "I do. I miss her, you know. Ouch! And that's not me intimating that you're a poor replacement, far from it. We're all lucky to have you on the team, and I'm even more fortunate to have you by my side as my partner. I never had a single doubt when Roberts ran the idea past me, you know."

Her partner turned briefly and her face lit up. "What if you hadn't wanted a Lorne mark two to work with?"

"I seriously believe I would be up shit creek right now. We're a force to be reckoned with, long may it continue."

Charlie wagged her finger. "But not if the consequences mean the destruction of your marriage, agreed?"

"Yep. I'd be lost without AJ and Georgie in my life. You're right on two counts. Firstly, I need to have a serious discussion with AJ about where we go from here, and secondly, I need to definitely delegate more. Rein in my enthusiasm and keep it under control. I never used to be a go-getter, not really. I think when Lorne first laid eyes on me, she despised me; I used to be so far up my own backside. You do know my history, don't you?"

"Umm… from what I can remember when Mum was cursing you back in the beginning, didn't you get the job because of who your father knew at the time?"

Katy laughed. "Yep, that about sums it up. I hope I've proved my worth by now, Roberts appears to at least be happy with the results the team delivers."

"You're an amazing leader. We all love working under you, take my word for that."

Katy looked in her direction. "Are you saying you guys are giving me marks out of ten?"

Charlie sniggered. "Hardly. Put it this way, if you were performing badly, I believe the knives would be out for you."

Katy almost choked on the laugh rising in her throat. "Tell it as it is, partner."

"I just did. Sorry, I shouldn't have opened my mouth. I meant it as a compliment. The team adore working for you as much as I do. I've learnt so much already. I'm still learning daily from how you battle through life and your duties at work. You're the strongest woman I know."

"Barring your mother, of course."

"Okay, yep, with the exception of Mum. Look at it this way, she wouldn't have handed over the reins if she felt you weren't up to the undertaking."

"Thanks for the pep talk, Charlie. I'll take on board the advice you've dished out today."

"Good. Please remember as well that I'll always be on your side, Katy."

Katy smiled and leaned her head back. "We do make a pretty awesome partnership."

"Long may it continue."

here was a positive sign when they approached the house, a large vehicle was parked on the drive which Katy presumed was mainly for Daniel's benefit. "Hopefully they're in."

"What if Megan is here?"

"We'll cross that bridge if we come to it."

They exited the car and walked up the path. Katy rang the bell and delved into her pocket to retrieve her warrant card. A grey-haired woman in her sixties opened the door.

"Hello. Can I help?"

Katy held up her ID. "Mrs Carr? I'm DI Katy Foster and this is my partner, DS Charlie Simpkins. Would it be possible to come in and speak to you for a minute or two on an urgent matter?"

"What on earth are you talking about? What urgent matter?"

Katy glanced over her shoulder and then leaned in closer. "It's concerning your niece, Megan. I don't suppose she's here?"

"No. She's at home. What's she supposed to have done?"

"Can we come in?" Katy urged a second time.

Mrs Carr motioned for them to join her and led them through the house to the kitchen-diner at the rear where a gentleman was sitting at the table alongside a younger man in a wheelchair.

"We're just finishing our lunch. Sam, these two ladies are from the police. They're asking me about Megan."

"Me Me!" The young man, Katy presumed to be Daniel, shouted.

Katy's stomach tied itself into knots, the last thing she wanted to do was upset the family.

"What? What do you want with our niece?" Mr Carr demanded. He pushed what was left of his roast dinner aside, leaned back in his chair and wiped his mouth on his paper napkin.

Katy's gaze settled on Daniel and then she turned her attention to Mrs Carr. "I don't think I should continue this conversation in front of Daniel."

"Why? Has something happened to Megan?" Mrs Carr said, fear emanating in her grey eyes.

Daniel wriggled in his chair and shouted, "Me Me!"

"It's Daniel's nickname for his sister. He's fine, he'll be okay, just tell us what's going on, you're scaring us."

"If you insist," Katy began only to be cut off by Mr Carr bouncing forward in his chair.

"No, I'm not liking the sound of this. I disagree with my wife, I don't think Daniel should be subjected to what you're about to tell us. I'll take him in the lounge, love. Let you deal with this."

Mrs Carr shook her head vehemently. "I can't, not without you, Sam. I can't deal with any further upset, we've had enough to contend with over the years."

"Please, we're only here to make enquiries at the moment. There's no need for either of you to become upset, although I do think it would be best if Daniel left the room."

Daniel angled his head and glared at Katy. His uncle wiped the dribble tracing a line down his chin. "I think it's best if we leave." He then wheeled Daniel out of the room.

"You might as well sit down," Mrs Carr instructed them. "Please, I don't want any hassle. My family have been through the wringer over the years."

Katy and Charlie sat down. Charlie placed her notebook on the table and flipped it open while Katy began, "I can imagine, taking on your niece and nephew at such a young age must have been traumatic for you?"

"We were happy to do it. I'm not saying our lives have been easy ever since, but our house has always been filled with love. The kids have grown into fine adults under our guidance. Now, perhaps you'll tell me why you want to speak with Megan?"

Katy glanced in Charlie's direction for a split second and then back at Mrs Carr. "It must have been hard taking on the responsibility what with Daniel's disabilities?" Katy asked, choosing not to raise the subject about Mrs Carr's niece for now.

"At first, yes, I admit, it was very difficult, but we've grown to accept life and the situation we're in as a family. We love this new version of him. I know you're going to find that hard to believe after seeing him, but you get into a routine. Our main aim in life now is to ensure he has an exceptional quality of life."

"That's admirable. Does Megan pop round to see you often?"

"Yes, a few times a week and regularly at the weekend, when she's not working."

"And where does she work?" Katy probed, homing in on the one fact that had managed to escape them so far.

"She works in a bottling factory on the production line. She hates it and has tried several times to leave the damn place but has been unlucky; each time the other job she had an interview for has fallen through at the last minute. She's a clever girl, she doesn't deserve to be slogging away in a factory."

"Has she worked there long?"

Mrs Carr paused and placed a finger on her cheek as she mulled over the question. "She worked in a café when she left school, but that closed down after a few months. That's when she saw the opening for the factory job. I warned her that it would be too mundane for her, but she wouldn't listen. She wanted a full-time job that would enable her to stand on her own two feet." She sighed heavily. "I told her there was no need for her to leave here, tried to tell her this was her home for however long she needed it to be, but she insisted she needed to get out there, to make something of her life. That's why the job at the factory was supposed to be a temporary measure. I think she's been there around four years now, waiting for another more prosperous opportunity to arise."

"Interesting. I'll get to my point, do you know where Megan is right now?"

"I'm guessing she's at home. Now, you need to tell me why you're so desperate to find her."

"There's no easy way to tell you this, but we believe your niece has been involved in some terrible crimes this week."

Mrs Carr gasped and covered her mouth with her shaking hand. After a few seconds, she dropped it and asked, "What sort of crimes?"

"The worst kind. We believe she's responsible for five deaths."

"What? This can't be true. There must be some mistake. Megan wouldn't... she doesn't have it in her to harm people. I think you've made a grave mistake."

Mr Carr appeared in the doorway. "Everything all right, love? What are they saying? Where's Megan?"

"Come in, Sam. You need to hear what they're accusing Megan of. It's unthinkable. It can't be true, I refuse to even contemplate it. How's Daniel? Should I go and be with him?"

Mr Carr entered the room and stood behind his wife. He placed his hands on her shoulders and massaged her neck. "He's fine. He's having a snooze."

"Good. I don't want him to hear this, it would kill him to know what they're suggesting of our... little girl."

"What's going on? I demand to know. You can't come in here accusing our niece of doing all sorts and not expect us to be upset."

"I appreciate you getting upset, the news isn't good, sir. We believe your niece is responsible for the deaths of five people. We're eager to speak with her."

"Wait! What? I can't get my head around what you've just told me. Back up a second. Five deaths? How? I want facts. How did these deaths occur?"

Katy nodded. She needed to tread carefully, so decided to leave the victims' names out of her summation. "Okay, the first death, the man was found in his car, it had been set alight."

"No way! Not Megan." Mr Carr paced the room.

"Love, take a seat and calm down. You and I know this can't be true. Let's hear what the inspector has to say for now. Let her speak without interruption." Mrs Carr reached for her husband's hand. He accepted it and gestured for Katy to continue.

"The second victim was knocked off his bike and run over several times." Katy watched the couple closely. Both of them seemed bewildered by what she was divulging. She continued, "The third man was attacked while he was taking a run through the forest. The three victims were specifically targeted."

"You mentioned five victims," Mr Carr said, frowning.

"We believe the man and woman found at the third murder scene were innocent bystanders, in the wrong place at the wrong time."

"Murdered?" Tears ran down Mrs Carr's cheeks. "Not Megan, she's not capable of murdering anyone. You're making a huge mistake, you have to be. Why do you think it's her?"

"Well, we believe it has to do with the accident that happened eighteen years ago."

The couple shared an anxious glance at each other. Then Mr Carr faced Katy again and asked, "What do you mean? She got over the accident years ago."

Katy cocked an eyebrow. "Did she? We believe she's been on a revenge mission. Megan has killed three out of the four men involved in the crash."

Mrs Carr let out a scream and sobbed. Her husband quickly tried to comfort her. "Hush now, you'll disturb Daniel and make him anxious. I don't know what to say. Is there any way you could be wrong?"

"We're ninety-nine percent certain Megan is to blame. There's more." Katy sighed.

Mr and Mrs Carr both stared at her. "What more could there be? Don't tell us she's gone after their families as well?"

"No, not yet. However, the final man, Ethan Romero…"

"The scum who was driving the damn car," Mr Carr finished off for her. "What about him?"

Katy sighed. "His eight-year-old son is missing."

Mr Carr sat back and dragged his gnarled hands through his greying hair. "My God, don't tell me that. Could this day get any worse?"

"I'm sorry to break the news, but as you can imagine, the family are at their wits' end and are desperate to get their son back home safely. That's why I need your help in trying to locate Megan. Can you think of anywhere she might go? Do you have a second home? A holiday home perhaps?"

"No, we're okay financially, but this house is all we have, anywhere else would need to be specially adapted for Daniel."

"Is there anywhere she liked to go as a child, maybe? Please, it's imperative we find her before she does something she might regret to the boy. He's an innocent party in all of this. If we can find her, it's possible we might stop her from making another huge mistake."

Mrs Carr wiped her nose on a tissue. "I understand. I swear, we would tell you if we could think of any likely places. We want Megan found as much as you do. You have to believe us, this has come out of the blue. We had no idea that she had such destructive thoughts running through her mind."

"Never in a million years would I have classed her as a killer," Mr Carr added. The colour had drained from his once ruddy complexion.

"Love, are you all right? You look a bit peaky."

He let out a shuddering breath and clutched his chest. "I don't know." With that he slumped in his chair.

"Shit! Charlie, ring for an ambulance." Katy loosened his tie and felt his neck for a pulse. She glanced up at Mrs Carr. "He's still with us. Does he have heart problems?"

"Not to my knowledge. Please, help him, he's always been a healthy man. Oh God, if I lose him, how will I ever cope? You have to do something." She frantically tugged on her husband's arm.

Katy unlatched her hand. "Mrs Carr, that's not going to help. You need to remain calm. Maybe you should go and check on Daniel, see if he's okay."

"Yes, yes, I'll do that. Take care of him."

"Of course."

Charlie finished her call. "They'll be five to ten minutes. Is there anything we can do to help him?"

"No, I'll keep monitoring his pulse, that's all we can do for now. Can you go wait by the front door for the paramedics, Charlie?"

"I'm on it. Jesus, what a day this is turning out to be."

A scream from the other room made Katy leap to her feet and tear after Charlie who had disappeared into the room.

"What's wrong?" Katy screeched.

Mrs Carr was leaning over Daniel and shaking his shoulders, tears streaming down her flushed face. "It's Daniel, he's unresponsive. I knew we shouldn't have left him alone. He needs an ambulance as well. Please, help us!"

"Charlie, wait by the door and make another call. Tell them to get their skates on for goodness' sake."

Her partner flew out of the room. Katy could hear a distant wailing of sirens a few streets away. Now they had a dilemma on their hands, who did the paramedics attend to first?

That'll be their decision when they get here, not mine, thank goodness. What are the odds on both men needing medical help at the same time? She rubbed her forehead.

Megan, you have a lot to answer for, not only because of the crimes you have committed, but also because of what you're now putting your family members through. Would you come out of hiding if you knew?

The question sparked an idea to run through her head. What if she held a press conference? Pleaded with Megan to come forward. Would she think Katy was trying to pull a fast one? Or would she take the plea seriously enough to give herself up? How much did her family really mean to her? Did she truly care about Daniel?

Katy observed the fear in Mrs Carr's eyes as she stroked Daniel's face. Katy tried to find a pulse in his neck, and she managed to find a slight one.

A paramedic burst into the room, carrying his bag. "Okay, step back, ladies. Can you tell me what happened?"

Mrs Carr filled him in. Katy left the room. In the distance, the sirens could be heard. *It won't be long now. They're almost with us. Hang in there, Mr Carr!*

The same paramedic who had dealt with Daniel came into the room and checked Mr Carr's vital signs. "He's faring better than the young man in there. We'll need to get them both on a stretcher and to the hospital immediately." He glanced up as Charlie joined them. "You ladies did well calling us immediately. Most people would have panicked."

"There was a certain amount of panic thrown into the mix, I assure you," Charlie replied. "What are their chances?"

"It's too hard to say. I've not dealt with many disabled people, they often have ongoing health issues which are hard to fathom unless you're a specialist. We'll take good care of them."

He went to find a colleague and they could hear them making arrangements with the other team of paramedics in the hallway. It wasn't long before a stretcher was being wheeled into the house and Mr Carr was placed on it. The other paramedics wheeled Daniel into the ambulance, still sitting in his wheelchair.

"I need to go with them. What I also need is for Megan to be by my side. Please, do your best to find her. She'll be devastated to hear what has happened to her uncle and her brother."

"Don't worry. I'm going to put out an appeal on the news, hopefully she'll see it and get in touch with us soon. I'll send a couple of officers to the hospital to be with you, just in case she shows up there."

"Will you give me your word you won't hurt her?" Mrs Carr pleaded pitifully.

"Of course. All we want to do is find her and make sure the child is all right. You go, we'll be in touch soon. Do you have your keys and some money?"

Mrs Carr ran into the kitchen and returned carrying her handbag. She slipped on her coat and smiled at Katy. "I don't know what I would have done if you hadn't been here to assist us. Thank you."

"Glad to be of help." Katy smiled at the woman. "Now go, we'll lock up for you."

"Thank you again." She walked out to the ambulances and decided to get in the second one holding Daniel.

Katy watched the woman get in the ambulance and groaned. "God, I feel so guilty now. If we hadn't—"

"Don't even go there, Katy. All we did was carry out our job. We couldn't have foreseen any of this happening. I'm sure both of them will be okay. We need to take stock and get back to the station, right?"

Katy patted Charlie on the forearm. "Too right. Let's lock up, you drive and I'll try and call in a few favours with the media."

*T*hirty minutes later, Katy had managed to get the all-clear to hold an emergency press conference. In attendance were journalists from both the written and TV media. She ran through the urgency behind trying to find Megan, stating that two of her family members were in hospital and that her aunt was desperately seeking her help in caring for them. She purposefully omitted mentioning anything about the crimes Megan had committed. Although she did add that Megan was likely to be with an eight-year-old boy.

It was a tough one to call, and she felt the wrath of Ethan Romero when the conference aired. "How dare you make out that our son is with this woman and is out on some kind of jolly with her?"

"I'm sorry, it was the only thing I could think of to get Megan to respond. If I had told the public that she'd kidnapped Matthew, there's no telling how Megan would have reacted. This way, I know I'm taking a gamble, but I'm hoping it'll pay off. Family is everything to her, it's unfortunate that her uncle and her brother have ended up in hospital, but I think that will work in our favour. All I'm asking is that you trust me on this one. There are many ways to skin a rabbit."

"It's cat," he snapped back.

"I know, but I never like to think of a cat being skinned so I adapted the saying."

Ethan grunted. "Whatever. If you screw this up, I'm warning you, you'll be personally hearing from my solicitor, got that?"

"I'm doing my very best to ensure that doesn't happen, sir. Was there anything else?"

"No. Keep me informed, if you don't mind."

"Of course I will. Have faith in my methods. I'm not guilty of doing things willy-nilly, I promise you."

He responded by slamming the phone down in her ear. "Bloody charming!"

Charlie leaned against the doorframe of her office. "What a dickhead. If it's any consolation, I think you've made the right call."

The phone rang again and Katy answered it. "DI Foster, how may I help?"

"How are they?"

Katy shot a glance at Charlie and ordered her to take a seat, then she put the phone on speaker. "Megan, is that you?"

"Yes," a timid voice responded. "How are they?" she repeated.

"I haven't checked since they were taken to hospital. Do you want to see them?"

"Yes, but I can't. You'll arrest me if I show up there."

"We won't, I promise. Come and see them, I'll meet you there. Your aunt could do with the support. She'll be torn in two down there, not knowing who to sit with for the best."

"Poor Auntie Gail. I never meant for them to get hurt." Her voice trailed off.

"Who? The men or your family?"

"My family. We've all been through a hellish existence since the accident. Daniel appears to be getting worse, at least that was my perception over the last few months. I needed to right the wrongs that had been committed."

"I totally understand the anguish you must have been carrying all these years, Megan. What about Matthew, where is he?"

"I haven't hurt him, if that's what you're thinking. I wanted to see that man suffer, the way my family has suffered over the years."

"The men were sent to prison, Megan. That was their punishment in the eyes of the law."

Megan grunted. "A few measly years behind bars and you think that wipes out the memories of seeing my parents lying in the car, dead? And also living each day with the consequences of the crash that my brother has to endure? It doesn't, nothing can make up for that, not even killing those bastards. I thought I'd feel better, but I don't. All it's done is compound my misery. My life is hell, but it's nothing to what my brother has to contend with day in, day out. No one cares about him, except for my aunt, uncle and myself."

"It might seem like that, but I assure you there are people out there who care about what matters to Daniel, I'm one of them. I was at the house, speaking with your aunt and uncle when they both fell ill." Katy noticed Charlie had closed her eyes and was shaking her head slightly. Katy realised then what a mistake it had been to inform Megan of that fact. She braced herself for a tongue lashing.

"What? You were there? Were you harassing them? You caused them to take a turn for the worst."

"No, it wasn't like that at all, I promise you. Your relatives asked why we are looking for you, the truth had to come out. Once they heard what you were guilty of, it knocked your uncle for six." Katy did her best to turn the tables on Megan, praying the guilt would make her drop her guard and surrender.

"In other words, you're telling me all this is my fault."

Katy rolled her eyes up to the ceiling. "No, I'm not saying that. I think it was a combination of things and the stress of the situation got to your uncle."

"And Daniel. What's wrong with him? I knew he was ill. I tried to tell my aunt and uncle, but they refused to listen to me."

"He's unwell, to what extent, we're unsure; we're waiting to hear back from the hospital."

"I want to see him, but if I show up at the hospital, you'll swoop, won't you?"

"I would allow you to see your relatives and then ask you to give yourself up. Where are you, Megan? Why don't you give yourself up?

Or at least, hand Matthew over to us. He doesn't deserve to be involved in this."

"Doesn't he? What's his father saying, is he showing any sign of remorse yet? Because since the accident, it has been severely lacking, even during his time behind bars."

"He feels guilty. He's fearful you're going to hurt his son, but I don't think that's your intention at all, is it, Megan?"

There was silence. Telling Katy that maybe the unbearable thought had filled Megan's mind after all.

"Megan, please don't do anything rash."

"I know, I know, he's an *innocent child.* So were we once upon a time before that damned crash. Before those men wiped out my parents and robbed my brother of any decent quality of life. Tell me why I shouldn't hurt him the way Daniel and I have been hurt over the years."

Distant sniffling caught Katy's attention. "Is he there, listening to this conversation?"

"Where else would he be? Don't worry, I've put him right on a few things. Did you know his father secretly told him about the incident, told him it was a simple accident? That he did nothing wrong stealing that car and driving it at over a hundred miles an hour?"

"He probably didn't want to scare his son, all he was doing was protecting him from the truth, Megan. He kept the incident from his partner. Perhaps, he was ashamed for what he did? And no, that's not me making excuses for him."

"Ashamed my arse. Like I said, he's never shown any kind of remorse. Never once reached out to us as a family to offer his condolences, neither have the others. Even when I watched the light fade from their eyes and they took their dying breath, those men didn't have the decency to utter an apology. The world will be a better place without them."

"Okay, there's not a lot I can say in response to that. What's your aim here, Megan?"

"My aim?"

"Yes, you have to have an ultimate goal? Why have you kidnapped Matthew if you have no intention of harming the lad?"

"That, Inspector, is for me to know and you to find out."

Katy's lip curled. She tried her hardest to remain calm, but the urge to shout at Megan was playing havoc on her tongue. "Megan, let's open a dialogue on where we go from here, shall we?"

"You can try."

"Do you even know? I'm begging you not to do anything rash, Matthew needs to be back with his family. You know how important that is, don't you?"

"Yes, we used to have a family unit that was strong and filled with love, once upon a time, until his father stole it from all of us. Maybe I'll break Matthew's neck, see how his mother and father cope caring for him when he's classed as paralysed. Maybe, just maybe, Ethan will find it in his heart to show some remorse then. What do you think, Matthew, shall I break your neck?"

"No. Please, don't hurt me." Katy's heart went out to the tormented little boy.

"Megan, you're better than that. Don't sink to Ethan's level. I doubt if you'd ever be able to live with the guilt. Answer me honestly, would you?"

"No. Maybe I have a get-out clause, an escape plan sorted to combat that particular issue."

Charlie frowned and whispered, "Suicide?"

Katy nodded. "You're talking about ending your life, aren't you, Megan? Why? There are people here who love you and who are relying on you for your support."

"Auntie Gail can carry on looking after Daniel, if he pulls through this. You know disabled people have a limited time to live, don't you?"

"No, I wasn't aware of that fact. Megan, we're going round in circles here. Please, come to the hospital, meet me there and we'll sit down and have a chat. Bring Matthew with you. I can get him home to his mother, think of her, of what this is doing to her. She's as innocent as her son. Don't make them suffer when your grievance is with Ethan."

"I don't want to get arrested. I did what needed to be done. People can't rob a family of their relatives and only be punished with the minimal sentence. It's not right."

"I get that. Come on, let's discuss how we can make things right."

There was a click on the line.

"Megan? Are you there?"

Silence.

11

"*P*lease, let me go. I want to go home."

Megan slammed the phone down hard on the table and stormed across the room to stand in front of the quivering boy. "You want, you want. That's all you kids ever say today."

She raised a fist to thump him, and he shielded his head with his arms and screamed.

The ear-piercing noise brought Megan out of her fury. She stepped back and apologised. "I'm sorry. Forgive me. I shouldn't take my foul mood out on you. That wasn't my intention at all."

"I need my Mummy and Daddy, please..." the boy sobbed. Snot running into his trembling mouth.

"You'll see your parents soon enough. Stop bugging me. I have to think."

It was imperative for her to change her plans. Her thoughts were all twisted, and she paced the floor in confusion. She needed to get to the hospital to see her brother and her uncle, but the risk would be too great to just show up there. An idea sparked in her mind.

Megan ran into her friend's bedroom. Lizzie and her fella Jamie had gone away for a week to Ireland to visit her parents as they hadn't seen them in over a year due to the pandemic. Lizzie was a student nurse, only started at the hospital around six months ago. She riffled through the rail in her friend's wardrobe, but failed to find what she was searching for. She stepped back, her five feet three inches not enough to see what might be tucked away on the shelves above. Megan raced across the room to retrieve the chair in the corner and dragged it into position. A glimpse of blue fabric caught her eye. She smiled. *See, it wasn't such a daft idea after all, was it?*

Yes, do it. Her mother's distant voice encouraged her.

Rummaging some more, Megan smiled when she located a long black wig. She threw the two items on the bed and continued her search. A dark blue cape should complete her ensemble. All she needed now was to find some flat black shoes and tights and her outfit would be complete.

After locating the required items, she went back into the lounge to find Matthew still bawling his eyes out. "Stop it. You're annoying me now, you wouldn't want to see me when I'm really angry, I promise you."

The boy instantly fell silent, apart from the odd sniffle. He wiped away the snot and the tears on the sleeve of his sweatshirt and stared at her. "What are you going to do with those?"

She grinned. "It's none of your business. Right, I'm going to have to leave you here while I nip out for a while."

"I don't want to be left alone. I'm scared."

She raced towards him, he flinched and shielded his face behind his arms. "Don't hit me."

Taking a step back, Megan stared at him. "Do they hit you? Your parents, do they hit you?"

His arms lowered and he nodded. "Sometimes when I'm naughty. I try not to be, but sometimes, I do really silly things."

Megan traced a finger down his cheek. "I'm sorry they treat you so poorly. If you were my brother, I'd care for you properly. Maybe when this is all over, you should seek help, speak out about the abuse you receive from your parents. I'm sick to death of hearing dreadful stories about parents treating their kids like punching bags. The world needs to get rid of parents who treat their kids so appallingly."

The loving way her parents treated her and her brother surfaced in her mind. A smile developed on her face. She shook herself out of her reverie and went into the kitchen to prepare the boy a sandwich. Cheese and pickle, that'll do, with a can of coke, that's what boys of his age crave for.

"Here you are, eat this. I'll be back before you know it."

"But I don't want to stay here, can't I come with you?"

"No, that's impossible. I have an errand to run, I'll be there and back before you've had the chance to say supercalifragilisticexpialidocious properly. Go on, give it a try."

"Super…what?"

"Supercalifragilisticexpialidocious." She almost broke into song. She didn't have time for this, to pander to the boy's whims. She needed to get to the hospital urgently. "Give it a try. If you succeed, I'll buy you a cream doughnut while I'm out, how's that?"

"Mum says I shouldn't have too many sweet things, it'll ruin my teeth."

"And she's right, silly me."

He chomped on his sandwich and let out a satisfied moan. "This is yummy. You'd make a nice mummy."

In spite of the anger bubbling inside, she smiled down at the boy. "One day, if that's what's in my future, I'd like to have a little boy, just like you. Now, I have to get changed. Be good."

He took another chunk out of his sandwich, and she left the room. In Lizzie's bedroom, she swiftly changed into the nurse's uniform and admired the result in the full-length mirror in the wardrobe. Luckily, they were the same size. She tucked the cape around her shoulders, slipped on her shoes and nodded. "You'll do. Let's hope the transformation will be enough to get past any police presence at the hospital."

She checked on Matthew one more time. He was trying to get his tongue around the long word she'd thrown at him; his attempt was poor, but he was having fun trying all the same. It would be a distraction for him in her absence.

"Wow. I didn't know you were a nurse. You look cool," he said through a mouthful of sandwich.

"It's borrowed. I'm not really a nurse. I'm going to the hospital to visit someone, which is why I need you to stay here and be good. Can you do that for me?"

His brow furrowed. "I think so. I'll do my best not to be scared. When my mum goes to the hospital to visit someone, she doesn't get dressed-up or change the colour of her hair."

"I like to look the part. Be good. I'll be back shortly, I promise."

*M*egan parked the car in a road near the hospital rather than pay their exorbitant fees just to have a space near the entrance. She entered the building and stopped at reception to ask what wards her brother and uncle were on.

"Are you new here? I haven't seen you around before," the redhead on reception asked.

"I work at another hospital, well, it's more like a care home for the elderly."

"Ah, is that Cedar Home?"

"Yes, that's the one. I thought I'd pop in and see my relatives on the way home from a long shift. I started at three this morning."

"I'm sorry, that's tough. Let me check the system, see what I can find out for you." She tapped the keyboard and then smiled at Megan. "Here we are, they're both in ICU. Take a left, hop on the lift and go to the fourth floor. Follow the signs when you get out of the lift and you'll soon come to ICU. Good luck, wishing your relatives a speedy recovery."

"You're too kind. Thank you."

She walked quickly and followed the route the woman had given her, arriving outside ICU within eight minutes. As suspected, she found two uniformed police outside the unit. She dipped her head, squirted on some hand sanitiser and pushed through the door.

Megan smiled at the nurse sitting behind the desk and drifted down the ward until she came to her uncle's bed. Her aunt wasn't there.

Her Uncle Sam's skin was grey, and he was attached to several IV drips and a heart monitor. She muttered a silent prayer and moved on.

It wasn't long before she located Daniel's bed. The nurses had placed him by the window, Megan presumed at her aunt's request. Daniel loved looking out of the window, watching the world go by from his chair. Tears welled and she placed a hand on her aunt's shoulder, startling her.

"My God, is that you, Megan? Oh gosh, it is you. You can't be here."

"I had to come. I'm sorry, Auntie Gail, none of this was supposed to happen. Everything got out of control. How are Daniel and Uncle Sam?"

"They're monitoring them both. The doctor thinks your uncle has had an angina attack. They're carrying out further tests on him. I should be with him. You should be here, helping me. I can't sit with both of them. I'm tired of caring for people. I've cared for Daniel for eighteen years now. I thought you appreciated what your uncle and I were doing for Daniel, but I was wrong. How could you destroy our family all over again?"

Tears surfaced at her aunt's harsh words. "I never meant to do that. Daniel has been getting worse lately, I could see that, even if you couldn't, and it got me thinking. The men who caused the accident are living life to the full and we're still limping along, caring for Daniel who is declining rapidly."

Disgust and confusion covered Gail's face. "None of this makes any sense, Megan. The lion's share of the caring falls on our shoulders, not yours. Why should it bother you to the extent it has done? How could you put us through this? Your actions reflect on this family. The police believe we're harbouring you. They think we know where you are, I told them we didn't and then you show up here, dressed like a damn nurse. I thought I knew you, I clearly know nothing about you or what foolish notions you have running through your head." Megan opened her mouth to object, but her aunt raised a hand to stop her. "I don't want to hear any excuses, I need to hear the truth. No more lies or deception, Megan." She sighed and looked exhausted.

"I'm sorry to have let you down, Auntie Gail. Something inside has been burning for years. I need to avenge my parents' death and what they did to Daniel. Look at him. You can't tell me he hasn't deteriorated in the past few months."

"I'm not denying that. The doctors are running constant tests on him, altering his medication to ease his pain. We need to give them time to find the solution, not take revenge for what shadows have blighted our past. I love you child, as if you were my own, but you've overstepped the mark this time. I'm not sure I want a damn killer in my life."

Her aunt's harsh words stung. Megan sighed and wiped away the tear that had slipped from her right eye. "I didn't mean to cause this much pain, not to you and Uncle Sam. I need you to forgive me."

"What you need, apart from a kick up the backside and a swipe around the head, is to turn yourself in to the police. There's a really nice inspector dealing with the case. I have her card at home. Go home and fetch it and get in touch with her."

"I've spoken to her already. She was on the news, appealing for me to come in. That's how I knew you were all here. I'm gutted it's come to this, Auntie Gail, but the wheels are in motion and I can't stop them until everything is dealt with."

Her aunt's eyes widened and she said through gritted teeth, "What's that supposed to bloody mean? Is it true what the inspector told me, that you've kidnapped a boy?"

She dipped her head in shame for a moment or two before her fighting spirit emerged from the doldrums. "Yes, and I'd do it again in a heartbeat to obtain the end result."

"My God, have you heard yourself? I don't know you at all, none of us do. You've been a stranger living amongst us all this time and none of us realised. What end result are you talking about? No, don't tell me, I think I can figure it out for myself, you're going to kill the boy's father, just like the others, aren't you?"

"I have to."

"Don't be so ridiculous, child. Who's telling you that?"

Megan placed a hand on either side of her head. "Mum and Dad, they've been inside my head for years. This is all down to them."

"Don't talk such rubbish. You need to put this right, Megan, give the child back and turn yourself in to the police. I hate our name being associated with a bloody murderer. How dare you bring such shame on our family? Do you really think your brother would have wanted what you've set out to achieve? No, I can categorically say he wouldn't. He'd be sick to the stomach, like I am, with the thought of those men lying in a mortuary somewhere. Their families devastated, as we were when your parents died. You're selfish, you haven't thought this through properly. Go to the police and give yourself up, for all our sakes."

Megan shook her head. "I can't. I refuse to do it. There's two more pieces to this puzzle. I'm sorry I've let you down, Auntie Gail. I did it for us, for Daniel. I don't care what you think of me. I'll be out of your hair soon enough. A disgrace to the family, that's what you're saying, and you're right. I am. But justice needs to be served. I intend to make sure that happens."

"You're not making any sense, Megan. These men served time in prison, justice has been served."

"Not in God's eyes. An eye for an eye. I'll ensure that happens." Megan refused to debate the matter further. "I love you all, never forget that," she called over her shoulder as she left the ward.

Her aunt didn't try to stop her. Instead, she remained seated by Daniel's side as usual. If only Megan could have drawn off her aunt's strength all these years. Her head was a mess, apparently, she no longer recognised right from wrong. Her parents lived in her head, guiding her movements. They were a constant form of comfort and demand on her at the same time.

She kept her head low and marched past the officers waiting in the hallway. One of them cast a suspicious eye her way. Her heart rate spiked until she rounded the corner at the end. Out of sight, she bolted down the hallway and jumped on the lift. As the doors closed, the officer appeared. "Wait! Megan, come back."

Shit! They know you're here now. You've fucked up, girl. Her mother's voice chastised her.

No, not necessarily. Her father chimed in. *She needs to leg it to the car. You've got this, Megan, we believe in you. Don't let us down now.*

"I've never let you down in the past, I don't intend doing it now."

The lift doors whooshed open. She squeezed through the gap once it was large enough and ran past the reception area and out into the fresh air. Sirens could be heard a few streets away. She had no idea if they belonged to an ambulance or a police car. Keeping her head low, she made her way back to her vehicle, casting an anxious glance over her shoulder every now and again.

Megan blew out a relieved breath once she was sitting behind the steering wheel. She drove away, her mind full of putting the final two pieces of the puzzle in place.

12

Katy and Charlie were just about to leave the station when the call came in. The desk sergeant raised a hand to prevent them from walking out the main doors.

"DI Foster, you'll want to hear this."

Katy took three steps and stood anxiously, awaiting further news in front of his desk. "What is it?"

She glanced nervously in Charlie's direction. Charlie appeared to be equally anxious and chewed on her lower lip.

Katy motioned for the desk sergeant to hurry up. "Come on. What's going on?"

He ended the call and released a long sigh. "My lads have touched base to say they believe Megan showed up at the hospital."

"That's great news, what am I missing?" she asked, noting his worried expression.

"She got away from them."

"What?" Katy shouted. "They had one frigging job to do and they failed to bloody do it. How?"

"In their defence, she was dressed as a nurse. One of my guys got suspicious as she walked past them, he chased her, but she lost him in the grounds of the hospital. All I can do is apologise."

Katy kicked out at the panel below the reception desk. "That's all we sodding need. What now? Was the boy with her? How long was she there? Did she see her family?"

"Watson said she was alone. She came out of ICU, so I'm presuming she must have spoken to her family or at least laid eyes on them. No idea how long she was there, do you want me to call him back to check?"

"No, it doesn't matter. The damage has already been done, she slipped out of our grasp and is probably now on the run. I just hope the boy is still alive and she hasn't dumped his body somewhere."

"Don't say that, boss," Charlie muttered. "What do you want to do?"

Katy kicked out at the panel again. "Well, that's put paid to us going home this evening. You can, but I refuse to let this lie. I need to be out there, searching for her, we're not doing any good twiddling our thumbs around here."

"If you're staying, then so am I," Charlie insisted.

"You're the best, Charlie. Come on, let's go back upstairs."

Charlie's brow furrowed. "I thought we'd be better off out there, searching for her?"

"We'll do that after I've fuelled up with coffee."

Katy was still fuming as she neared the end of her drink. She and Charlie had spent the last ten minutes bouncing ideas around.

"I suppose, going to her place of work is out of the question," Charlie suggested. She placed her cup on the desk and rose to her feet.

"On a Sunday, yes. Maybe we should have contacted them sooner. I'm at fault there. Everything escalated pretty quickly, catching us off-guard." Katy stood and stretched out the knots fusing her spine together.

"Where are we going to start the search?"

Katy shrugged and pulled a face. "Your guess is as good as mine. I think maybe we should head back to the hospital, see if the aunt can give us a possible list of friends we can try."

"If you don't mind me saying, that's unlikely, given that she was whisked away by an ambulance, she would have hardly thought to have grabbed her address book before she left the house."

Katy kicked out at a nearby chair and caught her shin. "Shit! I must stop doing that, it was only a matter of time before the chair took revenge." She rubbed her leg until the throbbing ceased. "We're wasting time hanging around here, let's go."

They rushed out of the station. On the way, Katy stopped off to speak to the desk sergeant to make him aware of their intentions. "Ring me if the slightest thing turns up, okay?"

"I'll do that, ma'am. Good luck on your mission."

"Thanks."

Katy and Charlie slipped into the car and Katy gunned the engine into life. She drove out of the car park, joined the flow of traffic and headed towards the hospital. "Keep your eyes peeled, Charlie."

"I will. What exactly am I looking for? She's already used several disguises to our knowledge, we don't even have a definitive picture of her in our heads, do we?"

"That's true. We're floundering, that's what we're doing. Maybe we would have been better off going home instead. No, I refuse to believe that. We're where we should be, out here."

Katy's phone rang, and she answered it on the hands-free. "DI Foster."

"Ma'am, it's Nigel back at the station. I thought you should know we've just received a call from Donna Platt."

"The boy's mother. What did she want?"

He sighed. "Her husband has been taken at knife-point by Megan Johnson."

"Fuck, fuck, fuck! How? I'll head over there now."

"There'd be no point. They left in his car. Megan had a knife at his throat."

"Jesus. I wonder where she's taking him. Okay, tell me you've put out an alert on the vehicle, Nigel."

"All in place. If they're out there, my guys will find them."

"I hope so. We'll keep trawling the streets. Ring me ASAP if you hear anything."

"That's a Roger."

Katy jabbed the button to end the call. "Bloody hell, could this day get any worse?"

Charlie didn't respond. Katy shot her a quick look and then returned her gaze to the road ahead. "Charlie, are you with me?"

"I'm thinking. All the victims were found in remote areas, right, what if…"

"What if what? Jesus, you think she's going to take him back to where the accident happened and do away with him there?"

"Just a thought. She's unstable enough to do it, isn't she?"

Katy flicked the switch and the siren blared. She thrust her foot on the accelerator with enough force their heads bashed against the head-rests. "I hope we're not too late. Do you know the exact location? I know roughly the area to aim for, but we need to be more accurate if we're going to find them quickly."

"I'll see what I can find out via the Net."

Ten minutes later, and with an accurate locale to aim for—thanks to Charlie's expert digging—Katy switched off the siren when they were within spitting distance of the site.

Charlie motioned ahead. "There's a car parked up at the end of this road." She studied her phone, matching it to the surroundings. "It looks similar to the photos. We're talking about nearly twenty years ago though, things change."

"People do as well. Right, get the pepper sprays ready and anything else you may find in my glove box." She smashed the steering wheel with the heel of her hand. "I should have signed out a Taser before we left."

"No time for recriminations. You're going to have to use your negotiating skills to talk to her."

"Jesus, I'm crap at that shite. I wish your mother was here, she'd go in all guns a-blazing, knowing exactly what to say and when to bloody say it. It can all be about the timings with something like this. Megan obviously has mental issues, if I utter so much as the wrong word, Ethan could be history."

Charlie touched her forearm. "You've just got to do the best you can. You've got this, Katy. You're better than you give yourself credit for, take my word for it."

"Thanks, I appreciate you having a considerable amount of faith in me."

"You're welcome. It's definitely them. I can see two people close together. Maybe we should pull up here and walk the rest of the way, it might be less threatening to her."

"You're right." She indicated and pulled into the kerb, then they both got out of the car and walked over to where Megan, still dressed as a nurse, was holding a knife to Ethan's throat beside the vehicle.

"Come any closer and I'll give him an extra smile," Megan warned, her eyes narrowed with intention. "What are you doing here?"

Katy and Charlie stopped and Katy raised a hand. "Megan, there's no need for this. Let him go."

"Who are you to tell me what I should and shouldn't do?"

"I'm DI Katy Foster."

"Ah yes, you were the one I spoke to earlier."

"That's right. I'm so glad we've found you before you make yet another mistake."

Megan's eyes narrowed further. "A mistake? Is that what you think this is? He was driving a stolen vehicle and killed two people, my parents, I suppose you'd call that a mistake or an error of judgement too, would you?"

"I'm sorry, how many more times do I have to say it?" Ethan whimpered.

Katy saw Megan's hold tighten around his neck, suppressing his windpipe until he started gasping for breath. "Megan, please, listen to me. We can get you and your family the help you need to combat any lingering issues you have concerning the accident, if you'll give me the chance."

"Any lingering issues? There are no issues. We've gone on to lead our lives as normal as possible, despite my brother's disabilities. I'm doing this for him, Daniel is getting worse. He should never have been put at risk in the first place. You weren't there, I was. This fucker deliberately drove at us, didn't you? I saw you, thought you were Mr Big in front of your friends. That day you had eight people's lives in your hands when you made the decision to play chicken with your own life."

Ethan choked a little and murmured, "I've regretted my decision ever since. I swear I have."

"Have you? You've gone out of your way to make contact with us as a family, to offer financial support? I don't think so. We've heard nothing from you and your so-called mates throughout the years. We've had to deal with coping with Daniel all this time alone, with just the crappy system to back us up. A system which is in desperate need of extra funding. No, all that went by with you lot, none of you were bothered. All you were ever concerned about was getting the best brief available to get you off on a lesser charge. I bet you're still paying off his fees now, aren't you?"

The knife nicked Ethan's throat and Katy found herself mesmerised by the trickle of blood running down towards his shirt collar.

"Megan, let's talk about this rationally. Don't be like them, you're better than that. What's done is done, it's time now to live your life the best you can."

"It's too late, I realise I've gone too far now. I have one more task to perform and I won't let you or anyone else prevent me from doing it. To this day, my family are still suffering. Daniel in particular." She angled Ethan's head to look at her. "Do you know he's in hospital right now?"

"No. I'm sorry, what more can I say?" His face belied his words, there wasn't an ounce of remorse visible in his expression.

"If I thought you meant those two simple words, then none of this would have happened, it's too late to feel sorry now. The only reason you're saying it is because I've got you pinned down and in a corner."

Katy noted how Megan's voice was tainted with hatred. *Keep talking to her, I have to try and make her see sense.* "Megan. Let him go. I promise you we'll do what we can to address the issues you have with the system. What will Daniel think of what you've done? Do you really believe he would want you to take retribution for something that occurred almost two decades ago? I doubt it. He needs you. What if your uncle doesn't make it? Your aunt is going to need your help even more then, isn't she?"

Megan appeared to pause for a second or two. "It's too late. I know what you're trying to do, to disarm me, to make me let this fucker go, it's not going to happen. He needs to die, just like the other three. They deserved it, but their deaths were quick. I wanted to prolong his death, his suffering, to make him really consider how much he'd wrecked all of our lives. My parents died when I was four, can you imagine the trauma I had to endure when I realised they'd gone for good? My brother died that day too, not physically perhaps, but mentally he did. My whole family wiped out because of this shithead."

Katy witnessed the darkness fill Megan's eyes. She sliced Ethan's neck wide open and let him drop to the floor.

Ethan gurgled and thrashed about for a few seconds.

Charlie gasped.

Crap, I know where this is leading. I have to step in. "Give me the knife, Megan," Katy ordered. She took a step towards the young woman, but Megan instantly placed the blade against her own throat.

"Come any closer and I'll do it. I need to watch him die, like I watched the others. You have no idea how satisfying it is to see. It'll never make up for losing my family, but it has gone a long way towards it, I can tell you. You should go now, there's nothing you can do for either of us."

"Megan, I'm pleading with you to think about your family, they need you, don't do anything rash. Think of them."

"I do. Every waking minute of the day, I'm thinking about them. You need to back away. To go. There's nothing for you to see here, not now."

Ethan spluttered blood and reached out a hand to Katy, then it crashed to the ground.

He was dead.

Katy's heart slumped. "Are you satisfied now? All of them are dead, they can no longer hurt you and your family."

A smile tugged at Megan's lips. She nodded and her mouth moved as if she was speaking to someone other than Katy and Charlie. Her gaze eventually met Katy's.

"I've done my duty. It's time for me to go. Don't try and save me. I no longer want to live in this world. I want to be with them."

Katy took a step forward, and Megan retreated a little. "Don't, Megan. Your brother, he needs you. Your aunt... her husband is ill, how will she ever cope caring for your brother and for him at the same time?"

"I can't think about that. My parents need me to be with them, I need to go to them. I've missed them. Yes, they've been in my head for years, but now, I have to be with them forever. It's my destiny. I couldn't go before killing these bastards, though. They had no right to live a life with no regrets."

"Megan, is there nothing I can say?" Katy pleaded.

"Nope." With that, she drew the knife across her throat and at the same time an angelic smile appeared.

Katy rushed to help her. She tried to stem the bleeding while Charlie called for an ambulance.

It was too late, the cut was deep, she'd successfully severed her carotid artery as intended.

"Jesus, no. Don't go. Come back, Megan!"

Charlie tapped Katy on the shoulder and shook her head. "It's too late, Katy, she's gone to be with her parents. It's what she wanted."

Katy's head slumped, she rose to her feet and stared down at the two corpses. Her frustration mounted. "I should have done better."

Charlie grabbed Katy's shoulders and shook her slightly. "Don't you dare blame yourself. She had an agenda which she was determined to see through to the end. She was brave to take her own life as well as theirs. Maybe the pressure proved to be too much for her come the end. The voices in her head, that of her parents, if you listened to what she said. They've been slowly driving her mad, it was inevitable her life would end this way. We need to stay focussed. Now, we have to think about the boy. We have to find him."

Katy shrugged. "How? We haven't got a clue where she was holding him. We need to check her flat."

"I'll get someone over there now." Charlie took a few paces to make the call.

Katy's gaze was drawn to the two corpses lying at her feet, and she shook her head. Defeated, the tears flowed and didn't stop until the ambulance appeared.

Patti arrived at the scene within half an hour. The first thing she did was to hug Katy and reassure her none of what had happened was her fault.

"I know. I'm tired, that's all. It's been a long week."

Patti placed a finger under her chin. "I've said this before and I'll say it again. You're a fantastic copper, but you need to delegate more. Your slim shoulders can't stand the burden, not all the time, hon, you hear me?"

"Are you in cahoots with AJ?"

"Nope. Go on, get yourself home. Sleep, you need sleep, everything should look brighter in the morning."

Charlie came to stand beside her and slipped an arm through Katy's. "We should go now."

"Take good care of her, Charlie."

"I will."

Charlie drove Katy home. AJ met them at the front door and Katy fell into his arms and sobbed. Charlie filled AJ in over a cup of coffee after which she called a taxi and went home, leaving them to it.

Once they were alone, AJ hugged Katy tightly. "I'm sorry if I put extra pressure on you today, sweetheart, that wasn't my intention. I had no idea what you were bloody dealing with."

"You didn't. That's not what this is about. I failed so many people today, most of all, I failed Megan. I should have saved her, and Ethan come to that. My negotiating skills were below par, I recognise that."

He gripped her shoulders and forced her to look at him. "No way. It seems to me like she needed to see her plan through to its conclusion. No one could have persuaded her to have taken a different path from the sounds of it. You can't go blaming yourself, love, I won't allow it.

You're a wonderful copper, even if your husband gives you grief from time to time for neglecting him."

Katy ran a hand over his cheek. "You're too good for me."

"Bollocks. We're good for each other. This was a blip, nothing more. Got that?"

He kissed her gently, emphasising his point.

EPILOGUE

*K*aty and Charlie were ordered to take the next few days off to get over the shock. DCI Roberts stood in for them and instructed the team to get started on finalising all the paperwork.

Katy spent two days in the arms of her husband who swiftly booked an impromptu few days away at a hotel, just for the three of them.

She watched Georgie thrashing about in the indoor swimming pool with AJ while she reclined on a sun lounger. The stress and tension of the last week virtually gone, finally. Although, what happened on Sunday and the gruesome scene she and Charlie had been forced to endure would remain with her for years to come.

On the Monday, Roberts had rung her briefly to bring her up to date. Matthew had been found at Megan's friend's house, when the woman had returned from her week away. He was now safely back with his mother, a blessed relief for Katy.

That night over dinner, AJ reached for her hand and kissed the back of it. "We're stronger than either of us realise. No matter what life may throw at us, Katy, we'll be sturdier at the end of it. We've been through so much already with Georgie. Nothing will tear us apart."

"I hope not. I promise not to get so involved in a case in the future that I neglect you guys as I have done this past week."

"Don't make any promises you can't keep, love. You're a determined officer, you should never change, Katy. I'm so proud of your achievements."

"But we need to spend more quality time together, right?"

"Yep, definitely. It would be a shame to miss out on Georgie's younger years, the way you have up until now."

"I know, believe me. I'm making a pledge to do my very best to change things in the future."

*K*aty and Charlie reported back for duty to what proved to be a hectic week. Katy had insisted they should attend all of the victims' funerals and also that of Megan Johnson. She was glad to see Megan's Uncle Sam out of hospital, sitting in a wheelchair next to his nephew, Daniel.

It was heartbreaking to hear Daniel calling out for his sister throughout the service. "Me Me, love you," he repeated, again and again.

Katy managed to steer Megan's aunt away for a quick chat after the service. "How are you coping, Gail?"

Gail stared at her husband and nephew and simply said, "I'm not. How could Megan do this to me? To us? I'll never be able to forgive her selfishness. She's blighted this family's name and left the three of us to face the dire consequences."

Katy rested a hand on her forearm. "Given time, people will forget."

"They might, but I won't. I'll never be able to forget. I haven't slept since I heard she killed herself. It was hard enough caring for Daniel, now I'm burdened with looking after my husband as well..." Her voice trailed off and she turned her back to blow her nose on a tissue.

"I'm sorry. If you need help, I can see what I can do for you."

"What I need is my life back, but that's not likely to happen, is it? Thank you for attending, Inspector. I'd better get back to my family who need me." She returned to her husband and nephew.

Charlie moved to within a few inches of Katy and nudged her. "She's hurting. I doubt if she meant all that."

"I wouldn't blame her if she did. I think she's been stretched to her limits. What an unforgiving world we live in. So many wrongs and not enough rights to counterbalance the scales. This was an emotional case for us to deal with, Charlie."

"I know. Let's hope we never stumble across something along these lines in the future. I believe it has taken its toll on both of us. By the way, Brandon and I had a serious chat last night, and fingers crossed, I think we're going to be all right. I've realised life is too short to give up on him."

Katy smiled, delighted by the news. She stared ahead of her and reflected on all the lives that had been affected by this case and let out a long sigh. "You're right, life is too short. Good luck to you, Charlie." She smiled. "Onwards with the next case, for our sins."

THE END

*K*aty and Charlie will be back later on in the year with another thrilling case to figure out.

*P*erhaps you'd also consider reading another of my most popular series? Grab the first book in the Justice series here, CRUEL JUSTICE

Or the gritty first book in the Hero Series TORN APART.

If you've enjoyed this book please consider leaving a review or possibly telling a friend.

. . .

hank you.

KEEP IN TOUCH WITH M A COMLEY HERE

Pick up a FREE novella by signing up to my newsletter today.
https://BookHip.com/WBRTGW

BookBub
www.bookbub.com/authors/m-a-comley

Blog
http://melcomley.blogspot.com

Join my special Facebook group to take part in monthly giveaways.

Readers' Group

Printed in Great Britain
by Amazon

57969590R00113